I0684829

Witches Blood

Nick Kisella

Based on the screenplay by

Ryan Scott Weber

First Printing

DEDICATIONS

Nick:

Kim, you and the twins are my reason to be.
Rich, here's another one-
To Ryan, Joe, Tom and everyone
that made the 'Mary Horror Trilogy' possible, including
the fans that have been such a big part of it all:
THANKS!

Ryan:

For my grandfather Ron Nardone. Rest in peace. Thanks
for everything you did for me. Kristen, for all of her love
and support. Thomas Brady, Brian Meehan, Joe Parascand
and Steve Ohlarik for all of their very hard work on this
film. To Nick who works his ass off to put out good
books. My dog Rocko for sitting by me while I edit.
Thanks to all the fans of this great series. It's been a wild
ride!

Witches Blood

CONTENTS

Witches Blood

PRELUDE

It was a late night at the radio station.

Gary Taylor was on his third cup of coffee

already, absently looking around the

broadcast room before his next show, which

he'd reluctantly agreed to do after his

regular shift.

"Money talks," he muttered to himself,

sipping his coffee.

Posters covered the room like colorful

wallpaper. He grinned when he saw the old photo of 'Zacherley the Cool Ghoul', a late night horror movie host, hanging directly across from him. Next to it was the real horror.

It was a flyer for 'Mary Horror Night'.

"I am so sick of 'Mary Horror'," He leaned back in his chair and sighed. "At least it's paying the bills."

Billy Lloyd walked into the studio. He was wearing his signature green windbreaker and had a bandanna tied around his head.

"On with the show," Gary said, putting on his radio persona with the flick of a mental switch.

The green 'On the Air' light blinked on

and Gary turned his microphone on.

"It's DJ Red here on 88.7 XFM. The last couple of years have been kind of tough for the town of Bernardsville, New Jersey. We had Mary Horror come back from the dead, and Sheriff Tom is wreaking havoc on the town. A zombie spell was cast on 'Mary Horror Night' just last week! Your own DJ Red has been through it all! We now have reports saying that Mary's spell book is still missing. It's somewhere out there, but we might have a man who knows where it is right now. Billy Lloyd was there and we have him in the studio tonight. Hey Billy!"

DJ Red waved at Billy and mouthed the word, 'Go'.

"Hey DJ Red! I'm a big fan!" Billy said

with a broad comical smile, waving to him. "I'd like to give a shout out to my buddy Jimmy," Billy was so nervous he was out of breath. "His name's Jimmy, and he's gettin' some action tonight!" He giggled, hands balled into fists, gyrating his body as if he were having sex. "It's a little pre-action before we go on vacation with our girlfriends."

"Wow, what a ladies' man." DJ Red put his head down for a second and rolled his eyes. "Now tell us what you saw just last week Billy."

"I saw some crazy shit." Billy sounded scared, stuttering out his answer. "Sheriff Tom, he had the book, and he went somewhere. I don't know where, and Mary, she was inside of my girl's body."

"Whoa, Billy! Well it seems like we're gonna get shut down by the FCC!" DJ Red said, half seriously. Thanks Billy for your time. And we do have reports of Sheriff Tom being sighted in the Salem, Mass area so, watch out Salem. Now here's 'Crash Romeo' with 'One hell of a time', on 88.7 XFM. I'm DJ Red."

ONE

It was an old dismal looking dirt road, quiet and untraveled. The morning sunlight glinted off the badge on Sheriff Tom's shirt as he walked, kicking up dust along the way.

When he saw the 'Welcome to Salem' sign in the distance he laughed harshly, and quickened his pace.

Sheriff Tom was well armed, with Mary Horror's spell book strapped to his belt and her cleaver in the tight grip of the Sheriff's left hand. He held the shotgun in his right. He'd used it so much in the past few weeks that it felt like an old friend.

He smirked when he finally passed the Salem sign, taking a deep breath and exhaling loudly. Suddenly his vision got hazy and his heart quickened. It felt as if a heavy weight had been dropped on his chest.

Sheriff Tom fell to the ground on the side of the road overcome with weakness. His body began to twitch and spasm painfully. He grunted and groaned, convulsing even more wildly, confusion and pain clouding his mind. The shotgun fell from his hand and he dropped the cleaver at his side.

As he slipped into unconsciousness, he

felt Mary Horror inside him, laughing.

Gradually, her spirit left his body.

Mary sensed the presence of a young blonde girl walking toward them in the distance. She was carrying her school books, taking a shortcut to get home.

She'd never get there.

Mary sends herself into the girl's body. When she has control, she looks at her new hands and a wicked grin forms on her lips.

Abruptly, Mary, in her new form, vanishes, only to reappear seconds later in a cloud of black smoke, right next to Sheriff Tom. She's in her white dress, still uncannily stained with blood from her previous encounters with the Sheriff.

The cleaver vanishes from the grass and

appears in her outstretched hand. The spell book, still on the ground at the Sheriff's hip, rises up and floats to Mary free hand.

"Thanks for the ride, Sheriff!" She said harshly, her body fading into a wisp of smoke, as if it were never there.

Moments later, Sheriff Tom sat up, fully awake. He looked down and saw both the cleaver, but more importantly, the book, gone.

"My book!" He growled, looking around frantically. "Mary!" He shouted, getting to his feet.

Holding his anger in check, Sheriff Tom retrieved his shotgun and continued on. The road was on a hill, above Salem. He crossed it and stared down at the town through a patch of bushes.

"Salem." He said gruffly, his good eye straining to see as much detail as possible. He found a narrow path that led directly down into the crowded streets and headed for the center of town.

He knew exactly where he was going.

Onlookers avoided him, surprised to see a man with an eye patch in uniform carrying a shotgun and casually walking through town.

The Sheriff carried on until he came to the house he was looking for from the top of the hill. It was surrounded by hedges. Rather than take the time to search for a gate, he shoved his way through them and approached the front door. He knocked several times, then stepped back when he heard someone coming to the door.

The man that answered the door was thin and slight in comparison to the Sheriff. He was dressed in a dark sweater, khakis and wore and Irish flat hat. He smiled, surprised when he opened the door, staring at Sheriff Tom.

"Oh my god, Thomas Walker! What brings you back to Salem?" He said with a hint of an accent.

"It's a long story, Jerry." The Sheriff's expression softened but his words were still edgy.

"Well, I don't normally answer the door when the devil comes knocking," Jerry said stepping outside, "but in your case I'll make an exception." He shook hands with Sheriff

Tom and nodded. "Please come inside." He said with a gesture to the door.

Jerry got them both a cup of coffee from a pot he already had brewing and sat across from Sheriff Tom in the living room.

"So Tom, exactly what happened to you?" His words were quiet, but his eyes narrowed on the Sheriff. "You look like you've been dragged from the bowels of hell."

"Hell is putting it lightly." Sheriff Tom's face stiffened and his words had a razor's edge to them.

"So I've heard." Jerry's eyes widened and he smirked at the Sheriff. "News of your exploits have reached even this small town. So why have you returned to Salem?" he persisted.

Sheriff Tom turned to face him, his good eye a narrow slit of anger.

"I need to know about Rebecca's spell book." He said, shaking a finger at the man.

"What about it?" The man replied, confused looking.

"It was mine." The Sheriff looked away in frustration. "It was taken from me. I need it back now!"

"Well, as the curator of the Salem Witch Museum I assure you, that book is nothing but trouble." He said firmly.

"It's my lifeline!" Sheriff Tom pounded a fist on the coffee table and stood up. His abrupt outburst sent the man back, pushing himself deeper into the couch. The Sheriff shook his head and pointed at the man. "She took it from me, and I feel weak without it."

"Who took it from you Tom?" He asked.

Sheriff Tom sat down again, his anger a fleeting moment.

"Mary." He replied flatly.

"She led you here didn't she?" He asked. "She manipulated you into coming to Salem because she knew that only in Salem could she inhabit the body of another host indefinitely."

"Oh you've got to be fucking kidding me." Sheriff Tom grumbled angrily, shaking his head in shock.

"Well, she is different now. She needs the blood of the other witches to make the book truly hers again, and once that happens, she'll be unstoppable."

"I've got to put a stop to this." The Sheriff said, his hands balling into fists.

"She's probably headed to Bernardsville right now. She knows she can't finish it in Salem, it wouldn't work." He rubbed his chin, deep in thought. "She needs to be close to the house where her family was killed. That's her permanent home now."

"I don't care, now that I'm this monster." He turned to face Jerry, a gleam of hatred in his eye. "I don't care if I have to kill everyone in my path."

"Y'know, there's a spell in that book that can grant you immortality." Jerry said staring intently at the Sheriff. "But once the witches blood is in it, you'll lose that opportunity forever. And once that happens, you have to revert to the man you once were." He stared off absently. "Or to the corpse you should be."

"I've got to stop her." Sheriff felt rage building inside him. "Enough, enough!" He shouted. He was about to stand again, but heard the echo of a news broadcast from a television at the far side of the room. Both he and Jerry looked up to watch it.

"Breaking news here. A special report. I'm Ronnie Pebbles for 'News 24'." The young dark haired reporter said, holding the microphone close to his face. He was standing in front of a railroad sign on the outskirts of Salem.

"Now it was reported earlier today that

Sheriff Tom Walker has been seen crossing

these railroad tracks behind me in Salem,

Massachusetts." A recent photo of Sheriff Tom

flashed into the corner of the television screen.

"That's right folks, so if you see Sheriff Tom,

he's armed and he's dangerous. Please report

him to the police."

Jerry and Sheriff Tom looked at each other.

"It might be wise for you to get a change of clothes." Jerry said calmly.

*****

Later that day Sheriff Tom was in one of Jerry's guest rooms. He was wearing a light blue dress shirt and dark pants. He felt strange not being in his uniform, a uniform that had become a part of him; but he was glad that Jerry had gone out and bought him some more discrete clothing while at the same time getting his old uniform cleaned and pressed.

He made sure the uniform was folded properly, as he always did it even before he'd fought Mary Horror and lost his eye, and packed it in a suitcase given to him on the bed in the center of the room.

Jerry's small dog, Rocko, was on the bed next to the suitcase playing with a bone. For a minute the Sheriff looked at the dog, envious of how carefree his life must have been, then he stumbled upon a photo that must have fallen out of his uniform and onto the floor when he'd changed earlier.

It was bent in half. He unfolded it and

saw that it was a picture of Arleen. Angrily, he crumpled it up and tossed it across the room. Without a word he grabbed the suitcase, his shotgun, and left the house.

Outside he got into Jerry's car. The keys were already in it so he started the engine.

"Tom listen," Jerry said, poking his head into the passenger side window. "Take care of this car for me, and good luck."

"It's all good!" Sheriff Tom said, laughing as he pulled out onto the street.

"I've got a bad feeling about this," Jerry muttered to himself, watching his car drive away.

TWO

George Banes was having a good day until he saw the news.

"Not again-" he lamented. It was more of the same old 'Mary Horror' stories, and he was not in the mood to hear about. He flicked the television off and headed upstairs for a relaxing soak in a hot tub.

He wasn't surprised when the phone rang while he was in the tub, but he was happy to be able to vent; even if it was only to a

reporter.

"I can't believe all this crap in the news.

This Mary Horror shit makes me sick!" He sat

up in the tube and shook his head.

"Why does it bother you so much?"

Chuck Marble asked on the other end of the

line.

"Well, embarrassingly, I'm her uncle, by

marriage." He chuckled.

"So you're really related to her." Chuck

asked.

"Yeah," George said dismissively.

"But since it's only through marriage

you're safe from the curse, right?" Chuck

tried to tread lightly on the aspect of the

curse. "Why does it bother you so much? Is

it all the victims?"

"Yeah, yeah. Because Bernardsville has been so terrorized." George said, feeling genuinely sad about the entire situation.

"Um, that's Bernardsville," Chuck said, correcting George for emphasizing the 'nard' in Bernardsville.

"Some people say BerNARDSville and some people say Bernardsville. What does it matter?" He replied, annoyed.

"Can you tell me about the whole witch thing? Were there other witches?" Chuck asked nervously, hoping he wouldn't get hung up on.

"It runs in the family. Well that's not all. My old auntie, I can remember her and my mom, showing off their spiritual skills when I was little. When I was growing up they'd always show off by making the table rise. They'd make the Ouija board answer questions without touching it. It was pretty spooky. I remember one night when I was really little, I had to pee in the middle of the night and I looked out the back window, and there they were under a full moon doing some weird ritual with a pentagram and that book."

"Did that frighten you as a child, to see them doing that?" Chuck asked.

"Yeah it scared the shit out of me." George leaned forward I the tub, the memory still making him feel uncomfortable.

"Have you ever told anyone about this?"

"No, I've never told anyone until now.

Lucky you." He chuckled and leaned back in the tub again.

"Do you think Mary had a normal childhood? I mean, could Arleen have been abusive or controlling and trying to get Mary to be like your mom and aunt?" Chuck asked.

"Yeah, and no. Arleen and Mary, they were very close. I don't think she would ever hurt her."

There was a knock at George's front door. He looked up and then looked at the phone. "Hey, would you hold on one second, I think someone's at my door."

George grabbed a towel, stepped out of the antique clawfoot tub, and headed downstairs to the door.

Just before he got to the door a stream of black smoke came up from under the door and suddenly a young blonde girl was standing in front of him holding a cleaver. She held the spell book he remembered so well from his childhood.

"Mary?" He asked, confused.

Before he could say another word, Mary hacked her Uncle George to pieces, cackling wildly.

Chuck heard the phone hit the floor, and then the laughter, and knew the interview was over. He doubted he'd even be able to use any of the material because he doubted that Mary's Uncle George was still alive.

*****

Billy Lloyd's room was a mess. There was

so much clothes all over the floor and furniture that it looked as if a laundry hamper puked.

"Jimmy this trip is gonna to be awesome!" Billy shouted, stuffing clothes into a backpack.

Jimmy, who was doing the same, turned and grinned at him.

"It is gonna be awesome." He laughed.

"Hey look, I've got the whipped cream," Billy said, releasing some air from the can. "Ya like that? See, I got condoms," he handed a few to Jimmy, "to protect our 'main veins', and baby oil, to lather up the women." He grinned, acting like he was smoothing oil on his girlfriend.

"Y'know somethin'?" Jimmy said, wide

eyed, "Where the fuck are the women?"

"They're probably doing 'girlie' things, right?" He replied, continuing to stuff more things in his backpack.

*****

Chuck Marble listened to the theme music of his new show beaming with pride. After all the turmoil he'd been through of late, the worst of which included being temporarily transformed into a zombie, he'd been promoted. He was given his own news program because of how well he'd handled all the drama that had happened in Bernardsville, covering it flawlessly.

He straightened his tie and smiled as the light on the camera in front of him flickered, signaling to him that he was live on the air.

"Hi everyone. I'm Chuck Marble, and thanks for joining us. As many of you know, it's been a very interesting last couple of years here in Bernardsville, New Jersey. Mary Horowitz moved into town in the summer of 2010 with her family from Salem, Massachusetts. She attended Bernardsville High School and she lived in the old Perkins house, which her grandfather, Marty Perkins, owned for several years. Well, on October 26, 2010 things took a turn for the worse in their family. Mary returned home after attending a football game to find her entire family slain, brutally murdered."

The camera turned toward a young man with black hair. He was dressed in a suit and wearing glasses.

"We're joined now by Dr. Handleford Crane, an expert on family tragedies. He's going to help us make a little more sense of this, years since it's happened." He turned to the doctor. "Dr. Crane, thank you for joining us."

"You're welcome Mr. Marble." The doctor nodded to him.

"Well several years have passed since the initial murders, you know, since that night, that was a horrific night for the Horowitz family. Ah, what do you think happened?"

"Well Chuck, Mary was lucky not to have been killed." He paused in thought, adjusted his glasses nervously and continued on. "Even though the murders were never

35

officially solved, there is no actual evidence pegging her to the actual murders themselves."

"I mean, who do you think is to blame?" Chuck asked.

"I believe it was her best friend Kelly, who was originally thought to be missed but later found slain on the front lawn of the 'Mary Horror' house. I'd also like to tell your viewers at home that I have a book coming out next week called 'Mary Happened' in which I explore all the theories dealing with Mary Horror."

"Mary Happened," Chuck smiled into the camera, "sounds like a good one. Please buy a copy if you can find it at your local bookstore. Its authored by our guest today,

Dr. Handleford Crane. We'd like to thank you Dr. Crane for being with us today. 'Mary Happened', his newest book. Please join us later as well because we'll be at the 'Mary Horror' house for a full report, all about Mary."

*****

Emma was driving Kristen through Billy's neighborhood, heading to his house where she knew he and Jimmy were packing. The windows were all open and music blared. She and Kristen were laughing and trying to sing along with the radio, wind tossing their long hair around the front of the car like soft auburn clouds.

Emma turned down the music and laughed, smiling like the cat that ate the canary at Kristen.

"I knew you wanted Billy's shit." She smirked.

"Whatever," Kristen replied, shaking her head. "What about you and Jimmy?"

"Jimmy's got balls, alright." Emma turned to her and smiled.

"Excuse me," Kristen said. "All I know is, I want to have a fun weekend. No zombies, I just want to have a good time."

"Yeah, I do too." Emma sighed, watching the road. "I mean it sucks, thinking about my brother Eric a lot, and Randall. I miss them a lot."

"I know, and I'm sorry. I miss them too." She said, staring off for a second before reaching into the bag down by her feet. "But,

I do have something, that you might enjoy."

Kristen pulled out a bottle of cinnamon whiskey and smiled. Emma's eyes widened when she glanced over to see it.

"Oh shit! Best friend forever!" She grabbed the bottle and looked it over. "For real!"

"Well, we all need to have some fun." Kristen took the bottle and put it back in the paper bag.

"How much you wanna make a bet," Kristen looked at Emma with one of her eyebrows quirked up, "that Billy brought the whipped cream."

"Ew, that's disgusting," Emma made a face.

"I wouldn't put it past him." Kristen shook

her head as Emma pulled over in front of Billy's house.

*****

"I can't wait Billy." Jimmy snickered, shoving the rest of his things into his backpack.

"Oh yeah," Billy echoed his sentiment, zipping his bag shut.

There was a loud knock on the door, and the two of them looked at each other smiling.

"Jimmy, they're here!" Billy, trying to stay calm, left the room to answer the door.

"Oh yeah?" Jimmy said, following his friend.

Billy pulled open the door smiling when he saw Kristen and Emma standing on the porch. They were both so pretty, thin and shapely, with long dark hair. They even wore bandanas wrapped around their heads just like he and Jimmy.

He still couldn't believe how much he and Jimmy had hit the jackpot when Kristen and Emma agreed to go out with them. "And now we're going on vacation together!" he thought to himself.

"Hello ladies," Billy said happily.

"Hey," Kristen said flatly. She nodded, and walked in.

"Who's ready to party?" Emma smiled, shaking the bottle of cinnamon whiskey.

*****

The 'Mary Horror' house was empty and quiet. Outside, the yard was immaculate. The town, knowing it was a tourist attraction, spared no expense in keeping it that way. The grass was cut regularly and the trees and bushes were always well trimmed.

A cloud of black smoke slowly materialized in front of the house. Its billowing darkness contrasting the green hedges it floated by.

There was an echo of laughter as Mary in her new body, coalesced in the smoke. Holding her cleaver in one hand and the spell book in the other, she looked at the house and smiled.

"It's nice to be home!" she said, laughing.

*****

Sheriff Tom hoped to reach Bernardsville in a few hours. He was driving nonstop, determined to get there as soon as possible.

His thoughts drifted while he drove, with memories, layers of images playing in his head like a high-definition film.

He remembered the day he found out the news that still haunted him. That scene in particular played out over and over in his head and he couldn't seem to shut it off.

The Sheriff was sitting in a doctor's office. Arleen was there with him.

"Well, what ya got doc?" the Sheriff asked, hiding how nervous he was in waiting for the answer.

"Well, after all the tested we did, we found out that Mary is indeed yours." The doctor, dressed in a crisp business suit said.

The information stung Sheriff Tom Walker

like a punch in the jaw, and that's when the memory took on a life of its own; twisting into a nightmare.

Arleen vanished, and suddenly there was a demented looking man in a lab coat to the right of the Sheriff. He was sitting there laughing.

"Mary's yours." He said, pointing a bony finger at the Sheriff. "You're fucked, fucked, bitch!" he cackled.

"Who the hell is this clown?" Sheriff Tom asked the doctor.

"He says he's a relative." The doctor replied. "From your wife's side of the family."

"I'm your brother-in-law, Dr. Bush!" the man said maniacally.

"Must be my ex-wife," Sheriff said, ignoring the man's further rants.

The doctor shook his head and looked at the Sheriff.

"So no chance of a mistake?" Sheriff Tom said, referring to the test results regarding Mary.

"No. Not unless it's one in a million." The doctor said firmly.

Sheriff Tom grimaced, and made a fist.

The cartoonish man in the lab coat that claimed to be his brother-in-law just laughed even more, pointing at him.

"You're fucked, fucked bitch!"

The memory abruptly ended and Sheriff Tom was staring at the road again, closer to New Jersey, and his mission.

*****

Billy snuggled closer to Kristen on the couch and he and Jimmy discussed where they wanted to go with their girlfriends. The news flashed on the television across from where they all sat on the couch.

"It's News 25! Here's Chuck Marble, with live breaking news."

The scene switched from the station logo to Chuck Marble standing in a wooded area between two men. They were both wearing camouflage jackets. One of them, bearded, looked like a Neanderthal. He was holding a long hunting knife, carried a crossbow and was chomping on an unlit cigar. The other was taller and had a thick goatee, with what looked like a coonskin cap on his head. He was leaning on a shotgun and chewing tobacco.

"I'm Chuck Marble. Something very strange is happening in and around the 'Mary Horror' house."

Billy and Jimmy went pale at the mention of 'Mary Horror'.

"Turn it up," Emma said nervously.

"Things are not over as we all expected them to be. We're just one week removed since our latest zombie-like incident, and we're joined here now by two men who claim they saw a Mary-like creature, or something, y'know, that looks very much like her roaming around.

"What the fuck?" Billy said, his heart skipping a beat.

"Hey, that's 'Hillbilly Jim' from TV."

Jimmy said, leaning back in the couch.

"No way." Kristen said shaking her head.

"You know him?" Jimmy asked.

"I'm talking about Mary you idiot."
Kristen said annoyed.

"They're talking about Mary as in 'Mary Horror'?" Emma said, pointing to the TV.

"That fucking cockblocking bitch!" Billy said angrily, fearful that somehow just the very mention of her name would ruin his time with Kristen.

"You saw something that looks like Mary in the flesh, running around?" Chuck pointed the microphone at the man chomping the cigar.

"Yeah, we were off huntin' in the woods, and some lady was there with a book and a cleaver. She went off that way," he said,

pointing to the left with his hunting knife. "She was real perdy."

"We believe Mary to be dangerous," Chuck said, "would you agree?"

"She was real perdy, but she did have a cleaver. What do you think?" The man asked his friend who was standing on the other side of Chuck Marble.

"Yes, what do you think?" Chuck said, swinging the microphone around to the other man.

"Yeah, we would a shot her, but I got scared and had some dingle berries so I reached around to scratch my ass and totally ran out of the woods."

"Wow. Ladies and gentlemen you're encouraged to stay in your homes. The Night

Hunters have been called. Please do not try to interfere with what they're doing. They are on the lookout for Mary Horror. Please do not come outside unless you absolutely need to do so. Chuck Marble, News 25."

The screen returned to the station logo, and an announcer spoke.

"The public reacts to the Mary Horror sighting."

The screen cut to a series of random people from around the town of Bernardsville.

"Oh shit, that crazy bitch is back?" a man standing in front of his house said, clearly panicked, "Fuck this shit, I'm leaving town!"

The station was able to 'bleep' out most, but not all of his cursing.

"Not even God is going to be able to help

us." A young woman with dark hair said fearfully, caught by the camera on the sidewalk in the center of town. "There is no God in Bernardsville! There's only Mary Horror, and she's coming to collect!"

A reporter even got someone to answer their door.

"No I'm not worried about Mary Horror." A heavy-set man wearing a baseball hat said, peeking around his front door. "I have real things to worry about. I'm a massive DVD, Bluray collector, and my collection is getting out of hand. I'm running out of space, I don't have places to put things; now that's a problem. Okay, this Mary Horror may be responsible for the disappearances of both of my twin brothers, but you know what? Both of *them are stupid, dumb fuckin' morons, and they got killed or whatever the fuck happened to them because they go and mess around with things that they have no business messin' around with. Now excuse me, I've got DVDs to look at." He slammed the door abruptly. Again, the TV station tried but failed to 'bleep' out all of what was considered 'foul language'*

"Yeah, I saw her." A teenager standing next to her younger sister said from their doorway. "I was kind of hoping she was gonna get her," she gestured to her younger sister, who turned to look at her angrily.

"Hey, that is not funny!" She turned and ran yelling for her mother.

"I was just kidding," she called out to her. "I gotta go," the older girl said, slamming the *door into the camera.*

The next person they showed was a man shouting as he sat in his car lighting a cigarette, but his language was so bad barely two words could actually be broadcasted.

The last person to flash on the screen was one of the notorious Night Hunters who had battled the zombies a few weeks prior.

"Yeah, I've heard of her." He said breathlessly. "Let me tell you something. I've hunted vampires, I've hunted demons, and I've even hunted zombies, but I'm not gonna mess with that witch. But you, you do me a favor. You see that Sheriff Tom, you tell him I've got something for him." He flung his long hair out of his face and turned away from the camera to get something. When he turned back he was

holding a long knife. "You tell him, the next time I see him, I'm gonna kill him! Now get out of here!" He held the knife close to the camera and grimaced furiously.

"There'll be more reactions to the renewed threat of Mary Horror at on News 25 at 11."

"We just got rid of all the fuckin' zombies, and now this?" Kristen said angrily, turning away from the TV to look at Billy. "I'm fuckin' moving."

"So much for a zombie-free weekend." Emma said wearily. "At least we got this." She held up the bottle of whiskey.

"Yeah, you know it baby." Jimmy smiled.

"We don't even know where Sheriff Tom went," Billy shook his head, "or what happened to Mary's body. I guess she got out or something."

"Who knows where Mary is." Emma said, twisting the cap off the bottle. "We should never have left there so quickly."

"We were in danger," Kristen said.

"We're the only ones that can save this town from catastrophe!" Billy tried to sound dramatic.

"Billy, we can kick some ass." Jimmy grinned.

A sudden knock at the door made them all jump. Billy shrieked.

"It's Mary's coming to fuck us!" Jimmy said, half seriously.

"Go, go check it out." Kristen said nervously, tapping Billy on the arm.

"Me?" Billy reluctantly stood up, Kristen pushing him away from the couch. "That was a loud noise." He said walking to the front door. "I'm scared," he mumbled, jumping back when he stepped on something that squeaked. He reached down a picked up a rubber duck. "Jimmy, you're leavin' your toys around again?" He tossed it at Jimmy and continued to the door.

Billy peeked through the curtain before answering the door.

"Holy shit!" He blurted out when he saw who was on the other side of the door.

He was trembling as he turned the doorknob and slowly pulled opened the door.

To everyone's utter surprise, Randall

stood there.

"It's a ghost!" Jimmy shouted, the girls crying out next to him on the couch

"Guys, it's me," Randall said, "I'm not a ghost, I'm alive! Let me in!"

Billy stepped away from the door and looked at her. When he was satisfied that she was there in the flesh he gestured for her to come inside.

"I can't believe it!" He said, returning to his spot next to Kristen on the couch as Randall sat down in a chair across from them. "We all thought you were dead."

"I was pretending to be dead so that Sheriff Tom would leave me alone." Randall looked at all of them. "When I got out of the lake, I went and found help. That person took me to the hospital. I had some water in my lungs. They said I had pneumonia, so that's why I was there for so long. I heard that you guys were going on a trip so I wanted to let you all know I was okay."

"We brought the book back to Mary's house like we said we were gonna do, but we never made it in." Kristen said.

"There was this crazy dude in a cape." Emma added.

"He must have lifted the zombie spell or something." Billy explained.

"Guys, where's Eric?" Randall asked, looking around.

The group looked sad. Emma started to get upset, but held it together.

"He's dead Randall." Billy sighed,

looking down. "Mary got him."

"What?" Randall was shocked, at a loss for words, but knew that had to be the reason why she couldn't reach him while she was hospitalized.

"Mary Horror's out there somewhere." Kristen said to everyone. "If nobody does anything, we're all gonna die."

"Wait, what's going on?" Randall said, confused.

"We're fucked." Jimmy blurted out. "The bitch is back."

"Well, it just said on the news that she's out there, with a cleaver and the spell book." Billy said.

"Well, we have to stop her." Randall said, angrily. "She took Eric. I always loved him.

I hope he knew that." Her words trailed off and she looked away.

"He did Randall." Emma said. "Here's to him." She spun the cap off the whiskey and chugged some right from the bottle, upset and disgusted with the entire situation.

"Jimmy we should go to your Uncle John's house." Billy said. "He knows all about, like, the spell books and the witch craft and all that shit, and he's really creepy."

"Uncle John likes to get his creep on." Jimmy laughed.

"If that old hag looks at me," Kristen looked at Billy. "I'm gonna punch him right in his face." She punched the palm of her hand in Billy's face.

"He looks me up and down, every time I

see him." Emma said, looking grossed out.

"Yeah," Jimmy said, looking her up and down himself with a smile.

"Don't worry baby." Billy put his arm around Kristen. "No one's gonna look at my girl."

Billy looked at Jimmy, then threw a fist in the air. "To the windbreakers Jimmy!"

THREE

Sheriff Tom was nearing Bernardsville. He wanted to shout in triumph, but was too plagued with mixed emotions caused by the snippets of memory still constantly flashing through his head.

He kept seeing the cemetery, and Arleen when she told him that Mary was his daughter, and then when his eye was torn out by that same daughter that he'd denied fathering. His back felt a twitch of phantom pain when he remembered the night Mary threw her cleaver at him, killing him. Then he remembered how he felt energy flowing through him as he was revived by the power of the book.

He felt like a pawn in chess game, and he didn't like it one bit.

"I'll show them!" He muttered, "I'll show all those fuckers!"

*****

The five of them got to Jimmy's Uncle John a couple of hours later. He only lived across town so Emma drove them all there.

True to form, Billy and Jimmy were wearing their green and yellow windbreakers.

Unlike Emma and Kristen, who had met Uncle John before, Randall hadn't; but she agreed with Billy; he was definitely a creepy man.

When they got to his house, he answered the door wearing ratty jeans and a short sleeved button down shirt that hung open to accommodate the ponderous bulk of his belly. Resting in the center of his chest, with part of it lying on his stomach, was a large wooden cross.

His hair was long, gray scraggly, and he had a white beard. If his arms and legs weren't so thin, Randall thought he would have made a great Santa Claus.

"Unreal, and he's supposed to help us?" Randall thought to herself, trying not grin or chuckle out loud.

Uncle John brought them to an attic room that had two couches, so they were all able to sit down facing each other. The girls were on one side and Billy and Jimmy sat on the other.

Uncle John stood between them, holding a large hunting knife.

"So Mary's back," he said, staring the knife, mesmerized.

"What is she doing back?" Randall asked, skeptically.

"She has to be back for her spell book," he replied, glaring at her as if she'd asked a stupid question.

"All I remember, is Mary's spirit coming out of my body," Kristen said warily, "and that little dude putting it back in the book"

"I think that Mary entered Sheriff Tom's body, that son of a bitch." Billy angrily pointed at Uncle John. "And then she came out, and she took the spell book."

"You must destroy that spell book!" Uncle John shouted. He pointed the knife at Billy and went on, "and in order to destroy the spell book, you need the correct spell, and the special item. You see, Mary is on a mission. She needs to gather the blood of all the witches that created that book, and infuse it, make it her own and put it into the book so that she may be powerful; all powerful. You see, without their blood, she'll be very weak." He looked at each of them. "Mary is whole again, and it's gonna get worse for you, gang."

Billy looked at Jimmy, totally freaked out by what he was hearing.

"So, we have to deal with more witches." Emma said, annoyed. She thought it was bad enough that Mary, a witch, had killed her brother, but now she'd have to deal with even more of them.

"She wants their blood." Uncle John confirmed. "There are four witches."

"Wait a second," Randall cut in, "there's four of them? I thought it was just Rebecca-"

"No!" Uncle John shouted, cutting her off and making everyone in the room jump. "Rebecca was only the last one to sign the book. She needs the blood of all four witches. Four witches created the book, four witches signed it. She needs the blood of all four." He turned to lock eyes with Billy, who leaned back, even more freaked out than before. "Without the blood of all four her power will slowly diminish. Yes, yes!" He ranted, staring up at the ceiling as if he saw something there, all the while getting louder. "Now that she's out of that house, she's growing weaker, weaker by the day. So she must act fast. She must perform the rituals, all the rituals, in order to get control of the witches and get their blood and control that book, and become all powerful and immortal and re-enter that house!"

For a moment, there was total silence, then Billy leaned over to Jimmy, rolling his eyes.

"What the fuck is wrong with your Uncle,

Jimmy?" He whispered, but everyone in the room could hear him.

"I don't know." Jimmy shook his head. "That's just how he acts all the time."

"I don't think we're coming to his birthday party." Billy said with a chuckle.

Uncle John ignored his comment and sat down, drained from his animated speech to the group.

"So what else do we have to do Uncle John?" Billy asked, hoping Uncle John didn't actually hear him earlier.

"You must find the lost one." He said dramatically. "The lost one that wears this necklace." He pulled a picture that was hanging up next to him down and handed it to Billy.

"That's her?" Billy said looking it over. "Hey, that's Pluto Lady, isn't it Jimmy?"

'Pluto Lady', as she was known around town, was widely regarded as a fanatic concerning Pluto and its status as a planet. She insisted it was still a planet despite what the experts said, and constantly harassed people with flyers and random speeches around town.

"Yeah." He replied with a smirk.

"She's an ugly bitch." Billy laughed.

"Never the less, that necklace that she is wearing can save your life. You need the spell too." Uncle John said cryptically. "I know that part won't be easy."

"The spell?" Randall asked.

"Yes, the spell that Mary's grandfather

buried in the back of that yellow house."
Uncle John said cryptically.

"Mary's house?" Kristen said nervously,
annoyed that she couldn't get away from it,
not even the house.

"Exactly." Uncle John nodded.

"How the hell are we gonna do that?"
Billy shook his head.

"Well, I have a map somewhere." Uncle
John looked at Billy. "Y'know, Marty and me,
we used to hang out."

Uncle John thought back to a day when
he and Marty were hanging out on the porch
of the big yellow house, Mary's house.

Marty had called him out of the blue and
made it sound urgent. It was a perfect night,
and Uncle John had already made plans, but

canceled them for Marty. He was sitting there smoking his pipe and Marty was just rocking in his chair, as if he'd never called him and they were just hanging out as they normally used to.

"I want to know why the hell you called me out to see you on a night like this." Uncle John said to Marty, annoyed.

Marty, who up until then had been staring off into the night, turned to face him. The shadows shrouded most of his features, and oddly enough, Uncle John thought he looked irate, almost evil.

"I'm giving this house to Arleen, and I'm moving out into the woods." Marty's words were low and gravely. "My wife won't let me have the spell book."

Marty thought back to when she had last called him to tell him their divorce was final.

"You can move to the house in New Jersey for all I care." She said angrily. "But you'll never get your hands on that book. I'm giving it to Mary, and that's it." She said firmly. That was the last time he'd ever heard her voice.

Marty remembered being so angry that he growled curses into the phone, unable to find any other words before finally ending the call.

"I tore out a page of the book and I hid it in the woods." He pulled a wooden box out from under his chair and handed it to Uncle John. "The map in this box will lead you to it. It's a spell."

"There's a map in this box, huh?" Uncle John gnawed on his pipe as he took the box from Marty.

"In case anything happens to me, that spell will destroy the spell book." Marty's eyes narrowed and he scowled at Uncle John.

"Yes, when he gave me this map," Uncle John said staring at Billy, "I never thought I'd have any use for it, until now."

He reached around and lifted the box up from the floor. Still holding his hunting knife, he lifted the lid of the box, flipping it open. The squeak of the hinges echoing eerily in the room.

"Oh yeah, here it is." He grabbed it and held it out in the light. "The little map. And as you can see, since you've been there before, the map is of the area behind Mary's house." He handed it over to Billy. "Who knows what else is back there."

*****

A short time later, the group was walking down a backstreet lined with trees. They all look tired and aggravated.

"I can't believe the car broke down." Randall shook her head.

"Uncle John will fix it." Billy smiled, trying to lighten the mood.

"Yeah, eventually," Randall snickered.

"I wonder whatever happened to Pluto Lady?" Billy asked, laughing.

"That weird ass bitch?" Emma said looking at Billy, who nodded. "She's having a party tonight, and people I know are going, though don't ask me why." Emma knew at least two guys from where she worked were going. They were a bit nerdy for her tastes, but she still couldn't understand why they'd want to party with Pluto Lady.

When Emma mentioned the party it was as if a light bulb had gone off over Billy's head.

"We can easily get the necklace, it would be so easy. C'mon, let's do it." Billy said excitedly looking at them all.

"We definitely can Billy." Jimmy agreed, smiling.

"Wait a second," Kristen said stopping in her tracks. "I don't know why I even hang out with you idiots. All we ever do is get in trouble. I'm better off going shopping or just staying home. I'm not puttin' up with this bullshit anymore."

"I think you like trouble." Billy said winking at her playfully.

"I think you need a tic-tac." Kristen said looking away annoyed.

Billy checked his breath and shrugged.

"We have no other choice." Emma said.

"Alright, why don't we just go to the party," Randall said, "We can get the necklace and get the fuck out. Hopefully we'll make it back to Mary's before sundown."

Kristen and Emma agreed, just wanting to get it over with.

"Alright," Billy went along with them. He waved Jimmy over as the rest of them walked past him.

"I got a plan Jimmy." Billy laughed. "It's perfect!"

"Alright, what is it?" Jimmy asked.

"Don't tell the ladies." Billy tried to sound secretive. "Do you like fire crotches?"

"Yeah, I definitely like fire crotches." Jimmy smirked wickedly.

"I think you should do Pluto Lady, and rip that necklace right off her." He grinned. "She wouldn't even know it!"

"You want me to fuck Pluto Lady?" Jimmy laughed.

FOUR

Later that afternoon, Pluto Lady was

indeed having a 'Pluto Party', Her small

apartment had posters of Pluto and signs that

read, 'Save Pluto' and 'Pluto is a planet' all

over the walls. There was even a little sign

posted outside that read, 'Pluto Party' so the

general public would know about it, and

hopefully attend.

Pluto Lady herself was wearing a 'Save Pluto' t-shirt. She was close to thirty, a bit on the curvy side, with light skin and long dark red hair.

There were five guys and one other girl attending the party besides herself. She was a bit disappointed at the turn-out, but that didn't stop her from speaking out for her cause, which she totally believed in.

All those in attendance looked like they were familiar with the terms 'nerd' and 'geek' just by the way they dressed and how they had such difficulty interacting with each other.

"Thanks you so much for coming to my 'Pluto is a planet' party." She said, raising a plastic cup, smiling. "This is in honor of my sister, who unfortunately passed away last week, to whom this cause was so important." Her brow furrowed when loud music from the apartment next to her vibrated the walls. "I'm sorry about the noise, but next door they're having another party about Neptune, they're really worried that it might be next on the chopping block." She rested her hand on a notebook. "Please, sign the petition to make Pluto a planet again, and have fun!" She implored enthusiastically.

They all cheered and Pluto Lady put on some music of her own, hoping it was loud enough to counter what was playing in the next apartment.

The guests mingled in their own way,

drinking what Pluto Lady called her 'Pluto Punch' as Billy and the rest of the group arrived.

Pluto Lady felt the alcohol she'd slipped into the punch start to hit. She felt flush and giddy.

*****

"I think this is it." Billy said, looking at a 'Pluto Party' sign on the wall next to the apartment door.

"Really?" Kristen said, rolling her eyes at him.

The group heard the last of her speech as they went inside, with Billy and Jimmy in the lead.

"Hello!" Pluto Lady said, her smile beaming as they walked in. "Welcome to my

'Pluto is a planet' party! Thank you for coming."

"I like getting real close." Billy approached Pluto Lady and put his arm around her. He rolled his eyes at Jimmy and tried to keep a straight face.

"Oh my fucking god, what is wrong with this bitch?" Kristen whispered to Randall. "And who the fuck has a party during the day?"

"Let's just get the necklace and get the hell out of here." Randall said, looking down so she didn't start laughing out loud.

"We really love Pluto, don't we guys? It's really good," Billy nodded to the rest of the group.

"Yeah, we love Pluto." Emma said,

stepping away from them to get a drink.

"Yeah we fucking love Pluto." Jimmy said, moving closer to Pluto Lady.

Billy saw the girls back off from them so he pulled Jimmy even closer to Pluto Lady and then switched places with him, putting Jimmy's arm around Pluto Lady in place of his own.

"Here," Billy said, pushing Jimmy into her. "She likes it."

"And don't forget to sign the petition over there." Pluto Lady said smiling. "It's for 'Pluto is a Planet'."

"Jimmy wants to show you something in the bathroom," Billy said, pushing them both toward the bathroom.

*****

The girls were drinking 'Pluto Punch' while secretly taking sips from the bottle that Kristen had brought. They were keeping to themselves, which left the remaining guests, the guys at least, nervous and quiet.

Billy was standing right outside the bathroom door. He knew that Jimmy and Pluto Lady were starting to get it on in there. He could hear them, and that meant everyone else could too if their antics continued to get louder. So he took that as a cue to liven things up, and couldn't think of a better to do it than his favorite pastime as a teen: breakdancing.

"Turn up the music, let's get this party started!" He shouted, comically falling to the floor and flipping into a spin on his back.

Everyone in the room began cheering Billy, his green windbreaker a blur as he awkwardly spun and flipped into different moves on the floor in the center of the room.

In the meantime, Jimmy was in the bathroom, having sex with Pluto Lady bent over the sink. They were both still dressed but had dropped their pants in the heat of the moment.

"Oh yeah, oh yeah, it's a planet!" Pluto Lady screeched, her hands white-knuckle gripping the sink as Jimmy slammed into her from behind. "Baby slap me with those Pluto balls!"

"Oh yeah! You like those Pluto balls, huh!" Jimmy shouted through gritted teeth. He could see Pluto Lady in the mirror above the sink. Her eyes were closed, and the necklace hung low from her neck, swinging back and forth. He reached around, and while acting like he was holding her closer, snapped the necklace off and slipping into the side pocket of his windbreaker.

After a rather overly dramatic finish, he sweet-talked Pluto Lady a bit, straightened out his clothes and then got out of the bathroom as fast as he could.

Billy had just finished breakdancing and met him at the door.

"Oh shit, you're done already." He chuckled, grinning at Jimmy.

"Yeah I'm done." Jimmy smirked.

"I was breakdancing." Billy nodded.

"How was it?" Jimmy asked.

"It was good. I still got it." He said seriously, suppressing a smile when Pluto Lady rushed out of the bathroom straightening her hair. "She's a little nutty, huh?" He nodded to Jimmy.

"Yeah." Jimmy grinned, straightening his bandana. "She definitely is."

"Wild ride huh?" Billy chuckled. "Did you get it? Did you get the goods?"

"Yeah, I got it." Jimmy put his hand in his pocket. "You want to see it?"

"Yeah, I wanna see what it looks like." He nodded.

Jimmy slipped the necklace out of his pocket. Turning away from the crowd in the room he showed it to Billy.

The pendent was circular, coppery

colored, with the symbol of the spell book engraved in white on the top of it.

Billy took it and looked it over, flipping it around in his fingers.

"Hm, looks like a nice round nipple," he chuckled. "Okay listen, I told Emma you were takin' a shit. She got drunk with the other girls and they went outside. I was a good distraction. Now let's go meet them outside." Billy slipped the pendent into his jacket pocket and led the way out of the party.

FIVE

Billy and Jimmy got outside and found

Kristen and Randall, neither of which looked

exactly sober, holding onto Emma, who

seemed ready to keel over. There was

another girl, Patty, standing by them eating

an ice cream cone. They knew her from the

Pluto party.

She was a short blond with pigtails and a high pitched voice.

Jimmy headed out to the girls but Billy stepped away because a solitary figure sitting on the curb looked familiar and caught his eye.

"Jimmy, come here." He said, looking pale and freaked out when he finally recognized the man sitting there. "I see another ghost Jimmy."

"I think it's, Eric?" Jimmy said, looking at Billy who's eye were bugged out.

Emma, looking a slightly more stable, pulled away from the girls and staggered over to Billy and Jimmy.

Kristen and Randall turned to see where she was going when they saw the man sitting on the curb.

"Eric?" Randall said, shocked.

"That's not Eric," Emma said, leaning on Billy's shoulder to steady herself. "This is Derek, his twin, my brother." She flopped down on the curb next to him and flung her arms around him.

"It looks just like Eric." Billy said looking at Jimmy and then Randall.

"This is a cruel joke, right?" Randall said, upset.

"This is Derek with a 'D'," Emma's words slurred.

Derek, looking surprised and slightly confused, looked up at them all and smiled.

"Hi," Derek said timidly.

"You want to help us? We're on a

mission." Billy asked. He held the map up. "This is a map, and this leads us to a spell that destroys Mary's spell book." He said excitedly. "She's out there, and we're gonna solve all the problems in Bernardsville." Derek looked at his sister Emma, her expression still an alcohol induced grin, and nodded.

"Yeah, we need to get some shovels, I guess right?" Randall turned away from Derek, because other than the scruffy beard he had, he looked too much like Eric to her.

"We'll need flashlights." Kristen said. "Flashlights will help too."

*****

The group returned to Billy's where they picked up what they'd need to follow the map and dig up the spell. When they got to Mary's house, they stood on the front lawn, staring at the house nervously. The memory of when they'd last been there still fresh in their minds.

"This place is fracking scary as frack!" Patty said, nudging her glasses up on her nose.

"I can't believe we're back." Kristen said, with Randall nodding in agreement.

"Let's just find the spell before it gets too dark." Emma whined, the alcohol still effecting her.

"Y'know, I wish we still had those guns." Billy said offhandedly.

"Where are they?" Emma asked.

"They're at home." Billy grinned happily.

"Billy, you're a pussy," Jimmy said, annoyed. "Let's just kill any motherfucker that's out there."

"You mean to tell me," Kristen said half laughing, "You remembered those stupid fucking jackets, and no guns?" She shook her head in disbelief while Billy smiled back at her.

"Hey, I like those jackets." Derek said.

"Thanks Derek. I really love my jacket." Jimmy grinned at him until Derek rubbed his shoulder, then he was slightly creeped out by the way Derek smiled at him.

"Either way, we can go into the woods, or we can stand out here, guns or no guns." Randal said, trying to ignore Derek's uncanny resemblance to Eric.

"Let's just find that spell," Billy said unwaveringly, "get that Mary bitch, and destroy that spell book so that I can go on vacation."

"Alright, let's go around the side," Kristen pointed to the right side of the house and they all headed off in that direction.

"Yeah, c'mon, before it gets dark." Randall agreed.

*****

Three members of the Night Hunters were in the 'war room' of their headquarters looking over a large map laid out across a table.

Dressed in their standard black uniforms, they had a serious dilemma on their hands.

"We have to find Commander Patrick!"

Mike, a brawny man with a shaved head and short beard said, slamming a fist on the map. "The last time he was seen was in this forest right here." He pointed to a patch of woods in Bernardsville. "He was abducted by a horde of zombies."

"What about Sheriff Tom?" Missy asked, flipping her long auburn ponytail over her should. She stood several inches taller than Mike, easily looking over his shoulder.

"Sheriff Tom?" Mike shook his head, locking onto Missy's striking blue eyes. "The last time we've seen him he was in Salem. But now that word is out about Mary being back in Bernardsville, we'll see him soon; because he's going to come, find her and kill her."

"Are you sure he's coming back here?" Heather asked. She was a mousey woman but a powerful fighter. "That area is swarmed and I don't want to risk the men."

"Well Heather, he's got no choice. He needs that book. It's his life's blood. We should be getting the whereabouts of Mary from our new commander shortly."

"What about Patrick?" Missy asked, concerned.

*****

Patrick was hiding out in an old barn, surrounded by zombies. He could hear them snarling, staggering around outside. He found a loose board in the wall and peaked through it, watching them lumber by in the darkness.

"They're everywhere." He mumbled through gritted teeth. "I can't stay here all night. I have to get back to the others. Damn you Tom Walker!"

Sheriff Tom had caused the zombies to appear in the first place, and all Patrick could think about while stranded in that barn was how he wished he could go back in time and kill him before all the insanity started, and the dead began walking around.

*****

"Can we use the big guns this time?" Missy asked Heather.

"These are the big guns," she replied, slapping Johnny, who had just come into the room, on the shoulder. He was holding an M16.

The sound of Mike's cell phone ringing made them all pause.

"Hello, " he said tersely. A look of relief came across his face. "We're on our way."

*****

The sun was going down. Somehow between sun glare and the loss of his eye, Sheriff Tom had missed the turn for the road that would have taken him into Bernardsville. He pulled onto the side of the road and got out of his car.

The anger was building up inside him and he wanted to scream at the coming darkness.

"Who fucked up these roads!" he growled, the irrational anger controlling him enough for him to believe it wasn't his own fault.

Suddenly a car pulled up close behind him. A well dressed man stepped out of the car and approached him.

Sheriff Tom let out and angry sigh and sat back down in his car, facing out.

"Excuse me sir, I'm Detective Blake. Is everything okay?" The man said, trying to get a good look at the man in the dimming light. "Is there a problem sir?"

The man lifted his head up. A chill ran up Detective Blake's spine as he recognized who the man was.

"Hey, aren't you that Sheriff Tom from the news?" He said, reaching for the pistol holstered in his belt. "I'm gonna have to ask you to stand up please."

Sheriff Tom abruptly stood up and grabbed Detective Blake by the throat. A low growl escaped his throat and he lifted the detective off the ground while squeezing his throat.

Detective Blake was hanging there in shock, struggling for a gasp of air, but feeling the steel-like fingers dig into his throat. The world became a red haze.

Sheriff Tom watched the life go out of the detective's eyes. Cursing to himself, he tossed the lifeless man to the ground, got back in his car and drove off.

*****

Chuck Marble started packing up his car after the last broadcast went out live. It was getting dark and he was tired. The fact that a rival station, News26 from Hawaii, of all places, was invading his turf by broadcasting directly across the street from them, made it all the more frustrating.

"Christ, they even had a girl in a bikini." He muttered to himself.

"Y'know Lonnie, it's great having you out in the field here with me tonight." Chuck said, shutting the trunk to his car. "Thanks for coming out."

Lonnie sighed, exasperated. Seeing their rival annoyed him as well.

"Thanks for having me Chuck." He leaned back against Chuck's car and loosened his tie. "I mean, it sure beats sitting in the studio with Marilyn the talking head. I mean, her body grew back and all, but I tell ya, ya take a woman out one time, and they don't shut the fuck up!"

"You know what we need to get the ratings up on this station?" Chuck said, inadvertently sounding like he was on the air again. "We should find Mary Horror ourselves. I think that would take care of a lot of things."

"Chuck, that's fuckin' right." Lonnie said so excited at the revelation that he slammed a fist into Chuck's car door. "Fuck News26, those stupid fuckin' Hawaiians! We gotta find her ourselves, yeah!"

"The 'Aloha Shirts', I mean I cannot fathom the fact that some 'Aloha Shirt' newscast with a bikini clad girl is gonna make our ratings go down. They're gonna go

down, maybe even close our station." He
shut his eyes and shook his head, frustrated.
"We cannot afford to get fuckin' canned, I've
already been through this! I mean, we need
to do something."

"Well Chuck, finding Mary Horror,"
Lonnie grabbed Chuck by the lapels and got
in his face enthusiastically, "does that give
you a boner or what!"

"Since you mentioned boners," Chuck
smiled and whispered in his ear as Lonnie let
go of him, "have you ever heard of the
'Manhole Club'?"

Lonnie leaned back and rubbed his chin
as if deep in thought, then turned back to
Chuck.

"No." He replied, suddenly looking very

uncomfortable.

*****

Sheriff Tom finally reached Marty's old cabin in the woods after nearly another hour of driving. He grabbed his suitcase from the backseat and let himself in.

The house was exactly as he had left it since the last time he'd seen Marty and picked up his weapons. With both Marty and his son dead, he didn't have to worry about anyone showing up, either.

"Time for Sheriff Tom to kick ass!" He said, changing into his uniform. It felt like a ritual, sacred to him.

"Back in business," he growled, after cleaning and loading his shotgun.

*****

The property behind Mary's house was larger than the group ever imagined it to be. The sun had gone down and they were still nowhere near their destination on the map.

Of course, that didn't include the time spent walking in circles because Billy and Jimmy were reading the map upside-down.

"You take it Derek," Kristen said grabbing the map from Billy and handing it to him. "These guys can't read a stop sign much less a map, and I'm sick of walking in circles!" She squinted angrily at Billy, and slapped his hand away when he tried to put his arm around her.

Billy looked at Jimmy and rolled his eyes.

"We have to keep going straight," Derek said, reading the map using one of the flashlights. "There's a split up ahead. I think we have to go left."

"Very interesting," Patty said nervously. She didn't like being out in the woods after dark, especially if there was a chance that either Mary Horror or Sheriff Tom could be nearby.

"Wait, wait," Billy said, urging them all to stop. He put his flashlight under his chin and smiled comically. "I want to tell you a scary story." He stuck his tongue out and smile. "No, really, I'm just lazy. I really want to stop walking and take a break."

"This brings back really bad memories." Kristen said, looking pale and upset. "I feel like a zombie can come out at anytime and attack us." She felt panicky, looking around wondering what was behind every shadow.

"I'll fuck those zombies up!" Billy said, jumping into a fighting pose, trying to make her feel better.

"Y'know, there could still be some out there, and we could die." Emma said, still thinking of her brother and how he'd died that last time they tackled Mary Horror and Sheriff Tom.

"Or explode." Randall said.

"I just exploded in my pants." Jimmy joked with a wicked smile.

Suddenly there was a loud moaning sound. It echoed through the trees all around them, and the group stepped back in fear, except for Emma.

"Oh my god!" She said, turning to face

them all with her arms outstretched. "Guys, there is nothing out here!"

Two arms suddenly grabbed Emma around the waste from out of the darkness behind her.

The group heard loud snarling as she was pulled into the blackness of the night, shrieking.

Emma was gone.

*****

The Night Hunters were in the woods nearby, searching for the barn where they knew Commander Patrick was hiding out.

"Missy, Heather, you go that way," Mike said pointing off to the right. "Johnny, you go that way, and make sure you check those corners." He turned back to look at the girls before they went off. "You okay?"

"Yeah, we got this," they both said at the same time.

"Okay, let's go." Mike said as they split up with him moving forward.

Sheriff Tom stepped out of the shadows behind them holding his shotgun.

"The hunters are now the hunted," he snarled through gritted teeth. "One by one, you're all gonna die!"

SIX

The back of Mary's house was a bustle of activity. News26 had just left and News25 had just pulled up. Marilyn Stone, a reporter that usually anchored the news with Lonnie Anderson was helping George the cameraman set up a couple of lights before they started their live broadcast. She was willing to do anything just to get out and away from the station for a while, but not away from Lonnie; and he was supposed to be reporting from the woods too.

When Handleford got there she straightened her skirt, checked her make-up and was ready to go.

"I'm Marilyn Stone, for News25. I'm here with live continuing coverage of our 'Mary Horror Sightings' story. We're here with Doctor Handleford Crane, who was just interviewed by Chuck Marble earlier today, and is an expert on all things Mary Horror. Dr. Crane, what do you think of all the latest news?"

"Oh my god, We're all going to die!" He was in a panic, visibly sweating. "She's a crazy bitch! She'll kill us all!"

"Calm down Handleford. What do you

think is the worst that can happen?" Marilyn asked, putting a reassuring hand on his shoulder.

"She'll kill all of us!" He stuttered. "I would stay in your homes people! The only thing that can save us is if that book gets destroyed! Mary must not be able to get in that house!" He pointed to the house behind him. "If that book is destroyed and she's in that house or even if Sheriff Tom is in that house, we'll have an even bigger problem on our hands!"

"What about zombies?" Marilyn quirked up an eyebrow. "Could there still be zombies in these woods?"

"Oh my god, I hope not! I hate zombies! Go out and buy my book "Mary Happened" and find out all the info you need to know."

A zombie quietly staggered up behind Handleford Crane. He heard it, turned and promptly passed out.

The cameraman screamed and ran off as soon as the zombie came into view.

The zombie turned and growled at Marilyn, ignoring the unconscious Handleford. She grinned and her eyes lit up. With a quick movement she ripped open her blouse, buttons flying all around, and shook her chest at him.

"Don't you want to get a taste of these?" Marilyn smiles at the zombie.

The dead man jumped at Marilyn and sunk his teeth into her neck.

"Oh yes! You remind me of Lonnie! I

love you Lonnie!" Marilyn shouts as her throat is torn open.

"Are the zombies gone?" Handleford stuttered, waking up just as Marilyn hits the ground, bloody and dead. He froze up and tried to scream as the zombie grabbed him.

*****

Billy and the group were still in shock after losing Emma. They tried to follow the zombie that took her, but it happened so fast and it was so dark out that they couldn't even find a trail.

When they stopped hearing Emma screaming they knew it was over, and moved on, not because they wanted to, but because they had to in order to finish what they started for the good of everyone. The dour mood echoed in the stillness of the night, with the crackle of dead leaves overly loud in the darkness as they continued on, not knowing what to expect, and in some ways, not caring anymore.

Billy had the map again. It looked easy enough to follow now that Derek had brought them most of the way.

"Just through these woods guys," Billy said, scanning the map with a flashlight. "Keep going."

He looked at Jimmy, who was right by his side. He was texting someone.

"Jimmy, who the hell are you texting?" He asked, annoyed.

"Tenikwa." Jimmy mumbled, nose still in his phone.

"Tenikwa?" Billy's eyes widen in amazement.

"Yeah." He replied benignly.

"Your girlfriend just died five minutes ago and you're texting another woman already?" Billy was exasperated at Jimmy, and part of him wanted to swing at him.

"Yeah, they like the 'hot rod'," Jimmy grinned.

"I know, and you like the curves, but come on, five minutes!" Billy said, angrily rolling his eyes.

*****

Heather and Missy, rifles poised for action, walked stealthily through the woods, careful of any sound around them.

"I can't see shit out here." Heather said

squinting. "It's not like we can use flashlights either, that'll just get us surrounded by whatever is out here."

The Night Hunters had recently lost their night-vision goggles due to a fire in one of their vans during the last zombie outbreak; making the mission they were on all the more difficult.

"I'm gonna look for Patrick over there," Missy pointed to the left with her rifle, "I'll meet you at the checkpoint."

Heather continued on, quickening her pace when she heard the familiar groaning sounds of the walking dead.

The murmuring wails of the dead were perpetually imbedded in her mind ever since her mother was torn apart by a small horde of zombies months earlier. That was what brought her to the Night Hunters, and her new life.

She saw one off to her right, arms flapping like ungodly wings clothed in a filthy white dress shirt, teeth bared at her.

A quick tug at the trigger of her shotgun sent the thing's brains as well as the top of its head raining on the ground like soggy confetti. She heard another and spun around blowing him away as well.

"That's for Mom," She mumbled, cursing under her breath as she moved on in the shadows of the night.

*****

Mike hadn't gotten more than twenty feet away from Heather and Missy before a walking corpse jumped out at him. He knocked it to the ground and shot it in the head just as another was coming up behind him.

The 'man' was a mess, covered in blood and wearing a wool hat. He snarled at Mike, lunging for him.

Mike shot one of his legs out from under him and then came the headshot, splattering the dark mess of brains on the ground.

Pointing his gun down, he quickly scanned the area and sighed deeply, wishing it was light outside.

*****

Missy was taking it slow but steady. She had the uncanny feeling that someone was watching her, but she couldn't see or hear anyone.

She slowed down even more, the darkness around her feeling like an entity rather than simply the lack of sunlight.

"Hello, is anyone there?" She called out against her own better judgment. By then she just wanted to get rid of the feeling that someone was there; needed to know that she was either truly alone, or at least had something to shoot at and destroy.

Missy got her answer, though it wasn't what she was expected or if truth be told, wanted to deal with by herself.

The sound of breathing, a harsh sound, came from behind her. She spun around on one foot, pointing her rifle up, but there was nothing there.

Then suddenly out of the liquid darkness he was there.

Sheriff Tom.

Her eyes widened for just a second before narrowing as she tried to aim, but the Sheriff was too quick for her. He snarled and moved like lightning, swinging a hunting knife, and slashing her across the throat.

Missy felt the wound, so deep it was as if her throat had been torn out. There was agony for a split second, then the pain was replaced by her struggle to breath, and then she slowly fell, her life spilling out through the hand she clutched at her throat with.

The last thing Missy ever saw was Sheriff Tom's face looking down at her.

"Get out of my way, bitch!" He shouted,

bending low enough to nearly touch her face.

When Missy stopped twitching, and the Sheriff heard a deep gurgling sound, he knew she was gone. With a snicker, he stood up and walked away, blood dripping from the blade he still held tightly in his hand.

*****

The News26 van stopped a few miles away from where they'd made their last broadcast across from Chuck Marble and his crew. They were still laughing about it when Larry, the cameraman stopped the van.

"Yeah, and the look on his face when he saw what I was wearing," Bikini Betty laughed, "it was priceless!"

"Let's just get this done so I can go home already," the cameraman grumbled.

Larry set them up in the woods near the Mary Horror house. It was pitch dark outside and they only had a couple of lights with them, so he could only wonder why they were even bothering.

"Aloha viewers, Bikini Betty here with News26." Bikini Betty smiled into the camera.

Betty had long dark brown hair, wore dark framed glasses, and had a pink leis around her neck. Her ample figure more than filled out the bikini she wore, which was brightly colored, especially under the light next to the camera.

"And I'm Hawaiian Ted, let's get laid everybody." He said, shaking the leis he also wore around his neck.

Ted was slightly taller than Betty, wore a small straw hat, a Hawaiian shirt and shorts. He was thirty, and clearly trying to act a part much too young for him.

"We're going into the woods tonight behind Mary Horror's house because we hear she's been running around. We're gonna find her for you," he pointed to the camera enthusiastically, "for our season finale!"

"I'm excited Ted," Betty said with a wide smile, posing sideways for the camera.

"Oh I bet you are," Ted chuckled.

Betty giggled like a little girl and stared into the camera, batting her eyelashes.

*****

Johnny stood in the shadows of a tree

waiting. He heard a gang of zombies off in the distance. They were moving in his direction so he wanted to get them all at once. Waiting patiently seemed like the only option.

"I hate being patient," he muttered, "I just want to fuckin' blow 'em all way and have a smoke!"

When they were close enough, he stepped out of the shadows and let the M16 do its job.

"Die Motherfuckers!" he yelled, shooting the dozen or so walking corpses to bits.

When it was over he leaned back against the tree again and lit a cigarette with a sigh.

*****

Commander Patrick heard gunfire

somewhere in the darkness. His heartbeat quickened.

"They finally got here!" He squinted out the opening in the barn. "It looks all clear out there, maybe I can find the rest of my crew."

He slipped out of the barn and carefully made his way in the direction of the gunfire he'd heard.

The sound led him over a hill, and there was a young boy standing there with his back to Patrick. It sounded as if the kid was crying.

Patrick wasn't sure what to do. He didn't exactly like kids to begin with, and he thought a sniveling adolescent would only cause him problems, but he felt bad.

"Maybe the kid lost his family tonight." He thought to himself, quietly approaching him.

"Hey kid, you shouldn't be out here," he said when he was in earshot of him. "You hear me?"

The crying only got louder.

"Are you okay," he asked, putting his hand on the kid's shoulder.

The boy turned around to face him. He was one of the dead, but there was something different about him, Commander Patrick could see that. He pulled his hand away just as the adolescent opened his mouth and spit flames at him.

Commander Patrick shouted in surprise, spun around on his heels and ran.

*****

Heather hadn't heard a sound since she left Missy and Mike. The further she walked, the more quiet things became.

She was bored.

"I look fuckin' good," she said, looking at herself on the screen of her camera phone. She started taking selfies.

"Mikey is gonna fall in love with you Heather," she went on, talking to herself and snapping more pictures. "Oh yeah, yes he is," she posed and smiled, "all the guys are gonna call you 'Heather Delicious'."

Sheriff Tom had been watching Heather all along from a safe distance. When she became lost in herself, he crept up on her and climbed onto a boulder right behind her.

Just as Heather saw the Sheriff come into view on her camera and started to turn around, Sheriff Tom struck.

He plunged the hunting knife straight down, right into the top of her skull, sinking the blade down to the hilt.

Blood poured out of Heather's mouth, nose and eyes at the same time as her body went limp.

"Heather Delicious." Sheriff Tom snarled, laughing maniacally.

He heard someone in the distance and froze. When he realized where the sound was coming from and who was making it, he kicked Heather's body off his blade and stepped down from the boulder.

Sheriff Tom approached the Night Hunter

silently as he rounded a few thick oak trees.

Mike didn't even have time to raise his gun to defend himself. He'd gotten around the last tree and suddenly the barrel of a shotgun was literally shoved in his face.

Mike could see Sheriff Tom directly in front of him holding the gun, smiling.

"You're fucked!" Sheriff Tom growled, firing the shotgun and spraying Mike's brains all around the grass, right where his now headless body fell.

*****

Mary Horror drew power from the shadows of the night. It fueled her ebbing strength and added to the energy originally given to her by the spell book.

She lit a fire behind the house deep in the

woods and called upon the spell book to summon three witches back into the physical world, with herself as the fourth.

She grinned triumphantly, a cackle of a laughter escaping her lips as she read a spell near the end of the book.

The initial summoning words were ancient, nearly silent, and the air around Mary grew still as she recited them. The symbol of the book glowed in her eyes, and she felt more alive than ever.

Energy pulsed inside her, throbbing in place of a heartbeat that hadn't existed for quite some time. She held out her hand and felt it flow from her fingertips.

"Rise my witches! Rise from the witches blood from which you came!" She shouted.

"Rise from the witches blood from which you came!"

The flames in the pit rose up in fury, the symbol from the cover of the spell book glowing even brighter in Mary's eyes.

The fire began to emit three separate trails of smoke, and the from the smoke, there came the witches.

Each materialized slowly, taking a form that mirrored one of the elements.

The first was like earth; with rough features, dark brown hair and tiny angry dark eyes.

The second was like air; thin, light of skin, hair nearly white, and eyes the color of a clear afternoon sky.

The third was like fire; curvy with deep

dark red hair, eyes and red lips that laughed

wickedly.

"My witches, we have much to discuss."

Mary said cackling evilly.

SEVEN

Billy, Jimmy and the rest of the group were slowly making progress to their destination. The flashlights were still bright, and Derek carried the shovel in one hand, leaning it against his shoulder, ready to swing if he had to.

A girl in her early teens jumped out at them from a patch of bushes and growled, teeth bared and boney fingers clawing at them.

"That's it," Patty stuttered fearfully straightening her glasses, "I'm out of here. I have a game of Q-bert to finish anyway. Patty, out!" She shouted, waving a hand at them all before turning and running as fast as her legs could carry her.

"What the hell is that?" Randall asked, staring at the girl in front of them.

"Hit her with the shovel," Jimmy said comically.

Kristen was so terrified that she froze, eyes wide, lower lip trembling.

"I love Q-bert." Billy said, staring off, "What a classic game."

"She's just a little girl, I can't hit her with

the shovel." Derek sounded upset, and shook his head out of frustration. "Let's just keep going."

"Okay," Billy agreed calmly, and they all ran past her without noticing Johnny sitting in front of a tree holding the M16, smoking a cigarette.

"Goddammit!" he said angrily, "I guess I better get this one too."

Johnny was about to stand up when Sheriff Tom came up on his left side.

The Sheriff smirked, feeling lucky to have found the last Night Hunter casually smoking a cigarette. He simply raised his shotgun and blew Johnny away before he even knew what hit him.

"That's the end of those Night Hunters!"

Sheriff Tom muttered, moving on.

*****

"I'm Chuck Marble live here in Bernardsville. We're coming to you live from the woods right near the border of Far Hills, and Bernardsville where we believe Mary Horror to be hiding out somewhere. Perhaps in a bush. Later tonight we will bring you live footage or pictures at least of Mary in the woods. We are certain that she is hiding around here and maybe-"

Lonnie cut him off, roughly grabbing the microphone from him and shoving him back.

"Sorry," Lonnie said to the camera, turning to face it. "What he's basically trying to say is Mary Horror is in the woods. She is in the woods, so stay away from the woods.

We'll do our best to get some live footage, but other than that; call the authorities to get to the woods! She's here!"

Lonnie turned away from the camera casually, and handed the microphone back to Chuck.

"See?" He said to Chuck. "See? What did we teach you?" He shook his head and walked away.

"Well thanks Lonnie. This has been Chuck Marble, News25."

*****

Mary Horror stood in front of the three witches holding the spell book and her cleaver. The fire had died down slightly, so they were all shrouded in shadows from the dancing flames.

"Ladies, you have been summoned here by me," She said sternly, "to defeat the one they call Sheriff Tom. Our witch beliefs are at risk!"

"Shall we tear him into two pieces, or three?" Rebecca, with hair like fire asked with a chuckle. She turned to the others and they all laughed together.

"No!" Mary said, running her finger up and down the edge of the cleaver. "You'll bring him here to me."

"Let's capture him, and make witch stew out of him," Rose, with hair as soft and light as the air said, giggling softly.

"Yes, I hope he isn't too salty." Sarah, with hair and eyes the color of the earth said. "I hope his flesh is sweet."

"We need to summon the army of the undead." Mary said with an evil grin. "We need to prepare for his attack."

"He'll have quite a surprise when he arrives." Sarah said, rubbing her hands together.

"We'll tear him to pieces," Rose said to Sarah, smiling.

They all laughed except for Mary, who momentarily turned away and rolled her eyes at their jovial banter. She had more sinister things in mind for them.

*****

Betty and Ted, with Larry the cameraman using a smaller handheld camera, were trudging through the woods trying to find Mary Horror. A loud moan echoed through the trees.

"What was that?" Betty said, jumping.

"I don't fuckin' know Betty," Ted grabbed her hand and started pulling her along. "Let's just keep going."

"What did you get me into Teddy?" Her voice was a nervous squeak.

"This bitch is weird," Ted muttered under his breath. As he continued walking, there was a horrible smell coming from behind him. He got nervous, thinking it may have been zombies or even Mary Horror and turned slowly.

The smell was coming from Betty.

"Did you seriously step in shit again?" Ted stopped in his tracks and said to her more annoyed than ever.

"Ted," she said, taking her glasses off and walking up to him. "You're the one that always shits your pants."

"I shit my pants one damn time!" He said, infuriated. "There was thunder and lightning! Just clean your fucking shoes!" He walked off shaking his head with the cameraman on his heels.

"I swear to god, if this bitch steps into another pile of shit again I'm going to rip my own head off! Let's just keep going Larry," Ted said to him.

"Okay, you're on." Larry said, pointing at Ted after turning the camera on again.

"Hawaiian Ted here, still in the woods. Alright, we've got to be close now." Suddenly he was distracted by a horrible smell again, and signaled for Larry to stop filming. "Cut, just cut." He said, wincing. "There's that horrible smell again." He turned to find Betty, but was suddenly overtaken by a handful of zombies. They knocked him to the ground and started tearing into him immediately.

Larry dropped the camera and tried to run, but was instead dragged to the ground next to Ted, who was already dead and being torn to pieces.

"Ted? Stop fooling around." Betty said, hearing all the commotion off in the distance.

Betty was still bent over cleaning off her shoe when a couple of zombies came up behind her. One of them literally ripped her ass off and then stuck her hand inside her and began tearing out her intestines.

Betty didn't even know what happened, falling to the ground dead before she could even scream.

*****

Patty had to slow down. Her heart was pounding so hard in her chest, and she was so out of breath that she thought she was going to collapse.

"I can't believe I'm one of the cool kids now." She said to herself after finally catching her breath. Hanging out with Billy and the group really made her feel like somebody, even if they were hunting after a dead witch and a bunch of zombies. "My Mom always said I was cool."

Out of nowhere came two zombies, one

on each side of her. One of them was a man and the other a young girl with pigtails. They both grabbed her.

Patty didn't realize what was happening. She roughly shoved the man away from her and screamed.

"Don't touch my boobs!" She shouted, not seeing the girl that still had her arm.

She shrieked again when the girl with pigtails unexpectedly bit her, and then Patty dropped her flashlight. The man jumped on her and between the two of them Patty was torn to pieces.

A homeless man was lying on the ground passed out a short distance away from where Patty was being feasted on.

"Mary Horror, zombies, witches," He

muttered waking in a stupor, sitting up with a bottle in a brown bag. "Crazy people running around." He noticed a small slip of paper on the ground and picked it up.

"What do we have here?" He stared at the paper, which as it turned out, wasn't just a paper; it was a lottery ticket. "Well this is my lucky day!"

The man stood up on wobbly legs and staggered off to the nearest liquor store to see if he was a winner and maybe pick up a fresh bottle.

*****

Commander Patrick ran into a horde of zombies just a few yards from the barn. He was out of ammo, and ended up punching a few and knocking them to the ground. He stomped on another's head, then raced back to the barn, his back against the wall.

"Damn!" He uttered.

He looked around in panic, seeing the sheer number of zombies around him and gritted his teeth. Out of the blue his cell phone rang.

"I finally got a signal!" His eyes lit up. He grabbed his phone and answered the call, noticing that his battery was very low.

"Patrick why don't you ever come to see me anymore?" He heard his grandmother say. "You don't even call."

"Grandma, how many times did I tell you, don't call me when I'm working!" He said into the phone. "My batteries about to-" He squeezed his eyes shut, infuriated when the call was disconnected. He pulled the phone away from his ear and looked at it.

"Dead, just like everything else out here." He looked around frantically. "Damn! Damn you all!" He shouted, leaping away from the barn in another attempt to make a run for it.

*****

Mary and the other witches were sitting around the fire, getting their plans straight.

"Mary, who is this Sheriff Tom that we must destroy?" Sarah asked, a glimmer of hatred in her eyes.

"He's been trying to stop me for years." She fed the fire and looked at Sarah, her eyes widening. "I feel this strange connection with him." She shook her head and looked at the fire. "He wants the book. We cannot let him have it."

"We won't let him" Rebecca chuckled.

"He's no match for all of us." Sarah added.

"We've been at this for many years." Rebecca smiled wickedly. "What hope has he?"

"Don't worry ladies, our army of the undead will do the dirty work for us." Mary's eyes glowed by the light of the fire.

There were nearly a dozen dead bodies lined up on the ground in front of the fire. Mary stepped away from the other witches and stood in front of the bodies, opening the spell book.

"These will add to the army I've been

building." Mary said to the others.

"May the army of the dead rise up and become whole again!" She recited from the book, her voice rising each time she repeated the phrase. "May the army of the dead rise up and become whole again!"

The witches behind her raised their arms, beckoning to the night sky as the bodies began to stir and rise up.

EIGHT

"You're all in my fuckin' way!" Sheriff Tom lashed out at horde of zombies coming right at him. He was surrounded, but fighting like a well-oiled machine. If he wasn't slashing them, he was punching them or shooting them.

He saw Commander Patrick downhill from where he stood, surrounded by the dead, and knew that's where he wanted to be. He hadn't realized there was one remaining Night Hunter alive, and wanted to quickly remedy that situation.

"Get out of my way!" Sheriff Tom shouted, smashing his fist into a zombies face, knocking it to the ground and out of his path.

He pulled out his shotgun when he reached Patrick, who didn't know the Sheriff was there yet and had his back to him.

"Don't move," Sheriff Tom said, cocking the shotgun right behind him.

"Sheriff Tom Walker, I knew you were still alive." Commander Patrick said, slowly turning around.

"Ready to die?" Sheriff Tom asked.

"Ready to fight?" Patrick held up his fists

angrily.

Zombies closed in on them, their snarling and growling echoing loudly around them. Sheriff Tom and Patrick saw it happening and suddenly took a different tactic. They both spun around and stood back to back.

"I hate zombies!" Sheriff Tom growled.

"Damn!" Commander Patrick said when he saw how many there actually were.

The two began taking zombies down, with Sheriff Tom using his shotgun and Patrick smashing them to the ground with his fists and then pouncing on their heads.

They took down most of them, with Commander Patrick confident that together they would finish them all off.

"Bring it on, bitches!" He shouted, taking

another down.

Before he could focus on another, Sheriff Tom impaled him through the back with the barrel of his shotgun. He felt the agony, looked down and saw the bloody gun barrel sticking out of his abdomen, then the blackness of death overcame him and his body collapsed, a lifeless heap.

Sheriff Tom kicked the body off his shotgun, stepping forward to watch it twitch and spasm on the ground.

"Shake, rattle and roll!" He snickered, moving on to take out more of the dead.

He was starting to feel weaker, and knew why.

"I've got to get my book!" He muttered urgently, running off into the woods.

*****

Chuck Marble and Lonnie Anderson were walking through the woods, trying to find Mary, or at least a trace of where she was or could be.

"What about Al?" Chuck asked Lonnie. "I mean, shouldn't we go looking for him?"

"No, we have cameras," he said, groping through his jacket, "well, I thought I had my phone. Well, we do need Al, because he's our fucking ride home!"

"Well, if that's the case we do need Al, but I do have my camera phone. Speaking of Al, and speaking of people that work in our news industry, I cannot stand that motherfucker at News26. Hawaiian Ted I think is his name. I'm gonna motherfuckin' kill him. I hate him."

"You know what," Lonnie said, putting his hand on Chuck's shoulder, "The sooner the better Chuck. I'm taking over his job."

"No fuckin' way!" Chuck was shocked. "You're goin' to News26?"

"Yep, I'm going to Hawaii!" Lonnie said.

"No fuckin' way!" Chuck couldn't believe it. He was a little annoyed that Lonnie hadn't confided in him up until then, but he thought that maybe Lonnie could help him get a job there as well. "Holy fuck! Well congratulations! Do you think maybe they can make me their lead news anchor now?"

"Do horses shit in the fuckin' woods?" Lonnie replied with a chuckle.

"I guess, yeah." Chuck said skeptically.

"Fuck New Jersey! This place sucks!" Lonnie said angrily. "I mean even the squirrels have STDs here."

"Well, I don't know if I'd know that, but congratulations." Chuck said, hoping Lonnie would actually be able to help him change jobs.

Suddenly a group of female zombies dressed to the nines was coming at them.

"Fuck no, go away please!" Chuck said as he and Lonnie jumped back.

Lonnie stumbled and fell flat on his back while Chuck turned and raced away as fast as his legs could carry him.

Lonnie stared up at an oncoming zombie and shook his head.

"Lisa?" He said, recognizing the dead

girl as an ex-girlfriend. The zombie bent down and got directly in Lonnie's face and snarled. "Baby, still swallowing I see." He sarcastically, knowing he was a minute away from being dead.

'Lisa' reached down and ripped right through his pants to tear off his testicles. Lonnie screamed in excruciating pain, watching the zombie raise his testicles in the air and squeeze them into a bloody pulp.

"You miss those balls, don't you," he whispered, going into shock.

The zombie responded by stuffing them in her mouth and chewing a few times. She spit them out in her hand and then shoved them at Lonnie, sticking them in his mouth.

Lonnie died trying to spit his own bloody

balls out.

In the meantime, Chuck was being confronted by another female zombie dressed in a black dress, her make-up smeared with blood.

"No! Here, you do the news." He shouted in panic, shoving the microphone at her.

She took it from him, and as he slipped and fell backwards pleading for his life, she stabbed right into his mouth with the microphone, twisting it around until Chuck died, choking on his own blood.

NINE

"Jimmy are we gonna get Taco Bell after this?" Billy said, stomping noisily through dead leaves.

"Subway's better." Jimmy nodded.

"Shut the hell up," Randall said, annoyed at how loud they were.

"Who farted?" Billy asked comically, "It smells."

Kristen just shook her head, frustrated

and scared. They were almost where they needed to be and all she could think of was getting it over with.

"I think we're getting' closer guys." Billy said, staring at the map again.

Zombies suddenly came out of the woods, surrounding them. Derek grappled with one using the shovel, knocking it to the ground and then smashed it in the head. Jimmy knocked one down and then kicked it.

Billy punched one in the face, sending it to the ground. He stood there, motionless, amazed at himself for doing it, then ran to catch up with Jimmy.

Kristen and Randall tag-teamed one. When it was on the ground Kristen recognized him.

"Oh my god, it's smelly Tim!" She said, covering her mouth with her hand.

"Y'know, I think Billy was right." Randall said, making a face. "He does smell like shit."

"Hey guys," Derek said, running over to them. "Billy and Jimmy went somewhere."

"We gotta go look for them." Kristen said.

"Yeah, let's go," Randall said.

They ran off trying to find them.

*****

"What the hell is happening Jimmy?" Billy shouted, huffing and puffing, trying to keep up with his friend.

"I don't know!" Jimmy yelled back to him. He was running as fast as he could, and ended up tripping up on a root sticking up out of the ground.

Billy pulled him up off the ground.

"Oh no Jimmy!" He shrieked. "Are you okay buddy? You can't die on me!"

"Yeah I'm all right!" Jimmy said trying to push Billy off.

"Okay, let's go sit on that stump over there." Billy said, out of breath and badly needing to rest for a minute.

They didn't see the homeless man a short distance away. He was holding the lottery ticket close to his eyes and trying to read off the numbers.

He noticed the zombies approaching a little too late.

"Aw hell!" he said, the dead dragging

him to the ground. He dropped the ticket

trying to push them off, but there was no

point in him even making the attempt. There

were too many of them and he was too drunk

to fight.

"Did you hear something?" Billy asked

when they got to the stump.

"Nope." Jimmy replied, adjusting the

bandanna he had around his head.

"Oh yeah, this is really nice." Billy said,

sitting down on the tree stump.

Jimmy tried to sit down next to him but

got shoved off by Billy, who took up most of

the space.

"C'mon, move your fuckin' ass." Jimmy

said, annoyed.

"Sorry Jimmy." Billy moved over to let

him sit too. "Those zombies must be leftovers from the spell last week. What do you think?"

"Yeah, definitely." Jimmy nodded.

*****

"I feel like Mary is deceiving us." Rose said to the other two witches. "Does she really need us to help her kill Sheriff Tom?"

"She's bad energy." Sarah said cryptically. "She is evil, and I don't trust her.

"Kill Sheriff Tom?" Rebecca said, "I didn't even feel she needed us to raise the army of the undead."

"We should get away from her. We're in a lot of danger." Rose said.

Before the witches could say anything else, they found themselves confronted by a hungry horde of zombies, with Mary leading them.

"Be careful my children, you don't want to tear them apart too much, I still need some of their blood!" Mary shouted to the horde, laughing maniacally.

The three witches knew they'd been betrayed, but had been taken unawares and were unable to fight back quickly enough as the mob ripped into their flesh and dragged them to the ground.

*****

"Let's get the hell out of here." Billy said, looking over at Jimmy.

"Well, all right." Jimmy agreed. "You want to go that way or this way?" He pointed off from where they came from as well as ahead of them.

"I'm not going that way with all the zombies. Fuck that shit." Billy said standing up. "C'mon, let's go. I've got the map right here." He and Jimmy both headed off in the other direction.

*****

"I can't believe we lost those idiots in the woods again!" Kristen said angrily.

"How do we even know that they went this way?" Randall wondered.

"Guys let's just keep looking." Derek said. "They couldn't have gotten too far."

They continued on for a while, and then Derek remembered something.

"Didn't they say that the Devil's Tree was somewhere up this way?" He asked.

Before either Kristen or Randall could respond, Sheriff Tom jumped out of the woods and lunged at them.

"Ya fucks!" He growled, forcing them to scatter. He grabbed Derek and flung him into a tree.

Derek, back against the tree, punched Sheriff Tom repeatedly in the face. The Sheriff just stood there grinning, the punches having no effect on him whatsoever.

"Ya better try again motherfucker!" Sheriff Tom said.

Derek punched him again, but it was no use, he was too strong.

Sheriff Tom punched right into Derek's chest, breaking through his ribs and grabbing his heart. He tore it free, pulling it out into the open, and squeezed it, blood squishing out on his hand and running down his arm.

Derek, eyes still wide with shock, slid slowly down the tree to the ground, blood seeping out of the hole in his chest.

Sheriff Tom saw the girls running away and took off after them. They had a head start, but he caught up to them quickly.

"Here, take this." Randall said, handing off the shovel that Derek dropped when Sheriff Tom grabbed him. "Oh my god, he's coming!"

Sheriff Tom lunged out and grabbed Randall around the waste. Kristen kept on running as Randall, being carried away, screamed in terror.

Randall was flung to the ground. She tried backing away but Sheriff Tom bent and grabbed her by the throat.

"This time you go out with a bang!" He shouted, holding his shotgun up to her head with his free hand. He squeezed the trigger and Randall's head exploded as she screamed, blood, bone and bits of brain spraying everywhere.

*****

"We are so close Jimmy." Billy said, studying the map. "It should be right up here," he said, looking up. "Oh my god!"

"What? What?" Jimmy asked, looking at him.

"It's a zombie Jimmy!" he said pointing. The zombie was wearing a suit, a very bloody suit, and coming at them fast.

"I'll hit 'em!" Jimmy said, grabbing a thick tree branch from the ground. He swung it at the zombie and missed.

"You better get your fists ready!" Billy said, holding up his hands like a boxer.

Jimmy nodded and together they each punched the zombie in the face. No matter how many times they hit him he wouldn't go down. It was as if he was just being stubborn, teetering on the edge, but refusing to go down.

"Oh god," Billy complained. "My stomach hurts!"

Jimmy hit the zombie several more times.

"Hey Jimmy, pull my finger!" Billy said comically, pointed his ass at the zombie.

Jimmy pulled on his finger and Billy farted long and loud, the rancid smell hitting the zombie and the dead man finally just fell flat.

"Oh yeah!" Billy shouted, "Lethal injection!" he pulled the map out again and showed it to Jimmy. All right, it's time. Fuck these zombies." He pointed ahead, "Let's keep moving."

They raced on for a bit, until Billy was too out of breath. He stuffed the map back in his jacket pocket and stopped.

"Jimmy, wait, wait, wait," he gasped.

"C'mon Billy!" Jimmy urged.

"I'm fat and I can't run that quick." Billy said still out of breath. "I'm tired! I'm tired and I just want to go on vacation! I'm tired of all these zombies and all this crap!"

"Don't be a pussy!" Jimmy joked.

"I'm just tired of it all Jimmy! I'm sick of it!" Billy whined.

Jimmy looked at their surroundings and suddenly knew where they were.

"You see this? This is the Devil's Tree, I think." He said, slapping the side of a wide dead tree in front of them. "It looks like it."

"This?" Billy asked.

"Yeah." Jimmy nodded.

"There's a giant hole in it." Billy looked at him skeptically. "This can't be it."

"Yeah, it is." He pointed to the map Billy was holding up. "Look on the map. It looks like it."

"It is it." Billy said, looking around. "I think this is where we're supposed to be."

"Are we gonna dig?" Jimmy asked, knowing they didn't have a shovel anymore.

"Did Uncle John say we had to dig?" Billy looked confused.

"I don't know what he said." Jimmy shook his head.

"I don't even know what he was talking about." He chuckled, "He had his shirt off and all, it was a little weird. I mean, I would think the person would come all the way out here and tired from running, they would just stick it in that hole." He put his hand on the rim of the hole in the tree. "I think you should put your hand in that hole. I bet you anything that the spell is in that hole, any money."

"I'm scared." Jimmy's voice cracked.

"Oh don't be a pussy, c'mon, you can do it." Billy tried to goad him into doing it.

"Why don't you do it.?" Jimmy asked, annoyed. "What about you?"

"Ah, I'm not doing that." Billy shook his head.

Jimmy just gave up, knowing it wouldn't happen unless he did it himself.

"Alright, here we go." Jimmy said, sticking his left hand in the hole.

"Get it in there good." Billy instructed. "Yeah, that's good." He said when he saw most of Jimmy's arm disappear in the tree.

"Oh, argh!" Jimmy yelled, "Ow, It's got me!"

"Jimmy, oh my god, Jimmy get your hand out of there!" Billy rushed over to him and tried pulling his arm out of the hole.

Jimmy shoved back on Billy and easily slipped his arm out of the tree holding a page from the spell book.

"I'm fuckin' kidding with ya Billy." Jimmy laughed, holding up the page he found inside the tree. "Here, I got it!"

"You're giving me a heart attack." Billy said putting his hands over his eyes. "It's the spell!"

"Yeah I think it is," Jimmy said looking it over with Billy, "isn't it?"

"Oh my god," Billy said nervously. "This is gonna end everything?"

"I think it is." Jimmy stepped away.

"Well alright!" Billy crumpled up the map. "We don't need this map anymore," he tossed it away.

The glint of metal caught his eye in the distance. He turned to check it out and his eyes widened.

"Oh my god, oh my god," Billy stuttered nervously, pointing. "Look, it's that motherfucker Sheriff Tom.

"That motherfucker!" Jimmy said angrily.

"You know what Jimmy?" Suddenly Billy looked determined. "Sheriff Tom, he must be going after Mary! She has the spell book. We can get the spell book, we can say the spell, and we can destroy it!"

"Sounds good." Jimmy said, hoping it was actually that easy.

"Good plan, right?" Billy's face lit up. "Then we can go on vacation."

Jimmy nodded. "Yeah! Let's do it Billy!"

"You think the girls will go topless?" He asked comically.

"Maybe." Jimmy smiled.

TEN

Sheriff Tom heard Mary's laughter ahead.

"Mary?" He called out in the darkness.

"It's got to be her," he muttered, running

toward the sound.

When he saw a fire in the distance he

knew she was there.

Mary was wiping up blood from the

second of the three witches. She was about to

get the blood of the last one when suddenly he was there.

"The Sheriff's back in town, bitch!" He shouted, standing across the fire from her.

Mary cackled an evil laugh, smeared two fingers in the blood of the last witch and stood up, blood on both of her hands. She also held the book and the cleaver.

"Ah, Sheriff Tom!" She glared at him, her eyes glowing with the symbol of the spell book.

Billy and Jimmy came running up, stopping at a stretch of bushes so they wouldn't be seen.

"Oh my god." Billy said, gasping for a breath after running for so long.

"Yeah Billy?" Jimmy said, coming up

behind him.

"It's Sheriff Tom, and Mary," He pointed them both out. He noticed that there was a group of the dead all around them just standing there, as if they were waiting.

"Yeah, there they are, the motherfuckers." Jimmy said staring at them.

"They have the spell book!" Billy said urgently. "We have to do something to distract them!"

"Well, just go get it." Jimmy pointed at him.

"I'm not fuckin' going out there!" Billy said as if Jimmy was totally insane for even thinking it.

"Give me my fucking book back!" Sheriff Tom shouted, holding out his hand.

"You know all I need is the blood of this last witch." She said as if beckoning to him. "Then the book will be mine." She started laughing.

"Say something," Jimmy said to Billy.

"What do you want me to say?" he asked, confused.

"I don't know whatever you want to say." Jimmy replied tersely.

"I think I'll kill you first." Mary held up her cleaver and started toward the Sheriff.

Sheriff Tom pulled out his hunting knife and did the same.

Mary reached him first.

"Let's go!" Sheriff Tom growled, ready to fight.

Mary still carried the book in her left

hand but had the cleaver in her right. She was ready to swing at him when they were both distracted by Billy shouting.

"Hey fuckers!" Billy shouted as loud as he could from the bushes.

Sheriff Tom caught on to the distraction first, knocking the book out of Mary's hands.

Billy and Jimmy both grinned when they saw that it landed near them.

"No!" Mary shouted, turning toward where it landed.

Sheriff Tom snatched the cleaver out of her hand before she could stop him or even move away.

Billy ran out into the clearing and grabbed the book, racing back to Jimmy, smiling triumphantly.

"You got the necklace?" He asked Jimmy, who pulled it out of his jacket pocket with a nod. "I got the spell! C'mon, let's do it!"

They ran off into the woods away from Sheriff Tom, Mary, and the dead that encircled them.

Mary sneered at Sheriff Tom, who now held both his hunting knife and her cleaver.

"Fuck you Sheriff Tom!" She shouted at him defiantly.

Sheriff Tom didn't say a word, he just pulled back his arm and backhandedly slashed Mary as hard as he could across the throat; neatly severing her head.

Mary's body fell backwards, hitting the ground, a twitching mess, and her head fell at Sheriff Tom's feet.

Out of the blue, Sheriff Tom's head felt like it was spinning. He became disoriented and confused.

Flashes of memory blinked in his mind and it was as if he was running through a shadowed nightmare of the past couple of years.

He saw Arleen walking away from him for the last time.

"Just forget it Tom, it's over. I can't believe you'd follow me to New Jersey." She said angrily.

Then he was standing in front of Mary's house before it was Mary's house; when her entire family was alive and still lived there.

He was in uniform and standing in front of Jeff, Arleen's husband. It was on what would be soon known as 'Mary Horror Night', but before the actual deed was done.

"Yes Jeff," Sheriff Tom said, walking up to the front porch.

"Thanks for getting here so quick Tom." Jeff sounded panicky. "I just got a call from Kelly. She backed out, she's in a panic."

"I told you about that bitch before didn't I!" Sheriff Tom shouted angrily.

"Hold down your voice, Arleen and my kid are inside." Jeff urged him.

"Sorry," He replied, shaking his head.

"What the fuck are we gonna do? Mary's gonna be home from the football game in about a half hour, and this has got to go down tonight. We're all depending it. Tom we're all depending on it. What the fuck are we gonna do?"

Sheriff Tom saw that Jeff was a total wreck, and he knew that everything they planned depended on what went down that night.

"I do her job, I get her pay." Sheriff Tom said, holding up the gun Kelly was supposed to use on Jeff's family.

"Put the fucking gun down, what the hell is wrong with you!" Jeff stuttered, pushing down on the gun Sheriff Tom was holding up. "Use something from the kitchen."

"Don't worry, I have something else in mind too." He squinted at Jeff, annoyed. "Now about my cut."

"Christ! Tom-" Jeff stood there shaking his head, knowing that he really had no choice. Everything was a mess because of his decision to use Kelly, which they were all against to begin with. He had to agree to Tom's terms no matter what they were just to get things done.

"Alright, alright," Jeff said nervously, "Ya got it, ya fuckin' got it. Just get it fuckin' over with!"

"Old Tom has to take one for the team." Sheriff Tom said, winking and turning away from him.

Sheriff Tom spun around in the woods, holding his head because it throbbed so painfully, like there was a spike going through it.

*****

Billy and Jimmy raced through the woods

until they found a small clearing. They didn't see any zombies in the area so Billy let himself collapse there, gasping for breath. He threw the book on the ground.

"Jimmy, give me the necklace Jimmy!" He said in a rush, pulling the spell out of his jacket pocket.

Jimmy fell to the ground next to him. He pulled out the necklace and handed it to Billy.

Behind them they saw someone running.

It was Kristen, and she was carrying the shovel.

"Oh my god, oh my god, you guys," Kristen said frantically when she saw them, "Sheriff Tom-"

"Kristen! Kristen you're okay!" Billy

shouted, relieved.

"Sheriff Tom's after us." She pointed to where she came from. "We've got to do something!"

"We saw him! We already got the spell book." Billy gestured to the items he had on the ground. "We've got the necklace, and we got the spell too. Jimmy and I found the Devil's Tree."

Billy wrapped the necklace around the spell book tightly. He looked at the spell and nodded.

"Okay, let's do this, let's end this crap!" Billy shouted.

*****

Sheriff Tom was still reeling, his head throbbing more than ever. The image of him standing in front of Mary's house, all dressed in black on the night that her family died flashed before his eyes, and he relived the moment again.

"If I can't have you, then nobody can!" Sheriff Tom said, pulling a black ski mask over his face.

He saw himself standing over Arleen as she took her last breath, and he remembered chasing Mary into the woods that night.

It was all him.

No matter how he tried to put it out of his head, he'd killed them all and ruined his biological daughter's life. He did it all out of jealousy and greed, and his head throbbed with the guilty pain of it all.

Only, it became worse after he'd become

a monster by his dead biological daughter's hand.

*****

"Here's the spell," Billy said pointing at the sheet of paper he held nervously. He started to recite it, still out of breath from running as well as excited to know that Kristen was still okay.

"Your time has come. Witches, zombies and all, disappear forever, disappear all!" Billy waited for something profound to happen, but there was nothing.

"Say it again, say it again!" Kristen urged.

As Billy recited the spell again, Sheriff Tom saw a flashback of Billy and Jimmy as paramedics finding Mary, and he, himself, tearing off the black ski mask by the trunk of his patrol car, when the ambulance pulled up.

"Fuckin' sirens," Sheriff Tom said, putting his hat on. "I hope she doesn't fuckin' survive!"

Sheriff Tom collapsed. He now knew that he had to get back to Mary's house if he hoped to survive. It was his lifeline, his anchor.

Fighting nausea, he used his shotgun to help get to his feet and ran unsteadily to the house. When he got there he climbed up the stairs of the front porch gasping as if he'd just run a marathon.

"Gotta get inside," he grumbled, struggled to go on.

As Billy repeated the spell, Sheriff Tom

could feel himself weakening, slipping away. He fell down the stairs, landing flat on his back in the grass.

Billy looked at the spell book and saw that it had begun to glow. He shoved Kristen and Billy aside then leaped away himself just as the spell book exploded into a ball of flames.

"No!" Sheriff Tom shouted, reaching up to the sky.

*****

Jimmy was the first to wake after the book exploded. It was still night and there was smoke all around him.

"Is everybody okay?" He asked, getting to his feet.

Billy started coughing, the smoke from

being so close to the explosion drying his throat.

"Holy shit Jimmy," He picked his head up and looked around. "I'm okay, I think! Now we definitely need a vacation!"

Kristen was behind him brushing herself off. She was glad everything was over and the book no longer a threat anymore, but she also thought the price they paid was much too high. They'd lost practically everyone they were friends with, everyone they cared about.

Nothing would ever be the same again.

*****

When they got themselves together a few minutes later, they just wanted to go home.

"I feel like I could sleep for a week!"

Kristen said, "And I can really use a good soak in a hot tub."

"Well, you'll have all the time you need when we're on vacation." Billy laughed.

"Yeah! Now we can really have some fun!" Jimmy said.

"Plus, I found this lottery ticket." Billy grinned, holding it up.

"Yeah?" Jimmy said.

"It's my lucky day." Billy said, continuing on through the woods with Kristen and Billy.

Together the three of them walked out of the woods, heading home. They passed Mary's house along the way. The sun was slowly starting to rise on a new day.

EPILOGUE

The DeLorean pulled into the driveway to Mary's house. The engine ran so smoothly that the only sound given off by the car was the crackle of the tires on the gravel driveway.

The beams from the headlights illuminated the front of Mary's house like twin spotlights at a circus.

When the car stopped, the driver's side door flipped open with a slight hiss and Billy stood up. He was wearing his green windbreaker and had a new bandanna wrapped around his head.

He turned to the backseat and helped Jimmy get out.

"C'mon Jimmy, you can do it." He said, practically pulling him up out of the seat.

Kristen got out of the passenger side and Tenikwa, Jimmy's new girlfriend, stood up out of the backseat on the passenger side.

"Whoa, that was tight Jimmy." Billy smiled, turning to look at the house.

"Yeah it definitely was." Jimmy nodded.

"Why the fuck did you bring us back here?" Kristen gestured to Mary's house, annoyed.

"What, it's Mary's house. Memories." He

said wistfully.

"But Billy I want to go on vacation."

Jimmy smacked him on the shoulder.

"Oh we will Jimmy, we will." He assured him. "Don't worry."

"Yeah, Jimmy, what happened?" Tenikwa said, confused. "I want to go on vacation, I'm all dressed up."

"Don't worry Tenikwa, we'll go on vacation right after this. I just wanted to stop by." Billy said.

"Why?" Kristen said, still annoyed at him for bringing her back to the house that was the object of so much pain and loss for all of them.

"Well, I have to tell you all something." Billy's face brightened and he smiled. "You know that lottery ticket I found after the spell book exploded? Numbers; 2, 3, 4, 5,6, and 9? Well, I won!" He held up a hand in triumph.

"Wow," Tenikwa's eyes widened in surprise.

Kristen looked at him skeptically, crossing her arms.

"I won, and this car," he pressed his hand on the roof of the DeLorean, "is not a rental. I bought it." He was so excited he couldn't stop smiling. "Guess what else I bought." He asked them with a smirk. "The house." He turned and pointed to Mary's house.

Jimmy shook his head, suddenly frustrated.

"I'm not fuckin' goin' in there." Kristen said, sounding more annoyed.

"Why not?" Billy asked, surprised at her answer. "It's beautiful."

"It's spooky." Tenikwa said with a nod.

"It's yellow." Jimmy waved his hand at the house dismissively.

"Yeah, just like Jimmy's jacket-" Billy turned and saw that Jimmy wasn't wearing his yellow windbreaker. "What the hell Jimmy! You're not wearing the yellow jacket! I'm wearing the green. We're supposed to wear them all the time!"

"I don't know," Jimmy shook his head slightly annoyed.

"Well, don't worry, I bought 365 of them. They're all inside. I got green, I got yellow and if you really want to go crazy I got red. Ya wanna go inside and check it out?" He asked Kristen.

"No." she said flatly, her eyes angry.

"Let's do it!" He said anyway, walking to the front door with Jimmy close behind. "It's all good." He looked back at Jimmy, "Didn't someone say that once, 'It's all good'?"

Kristen looked back at Tenikwa, who threw her hands up in the air, flabbergasted. In spite of her misgivings Kristen followed with Tenikwa close behind.

"Oh my god, I can't wait for you guys to see-" Billy turned around as he got to the front door and saw that the three of them were waiting by the steps, not even wanting to walk on the porch.

"C'mon!" Billy pleaded, annoyed. "Don't you want to go on vacation? I gotta show you the inside. It's awesome!" He flipped the

front door open.

Sheriff Tom was standing in the doorway

holding up his hunting knife.

"It's all good!" He shouted, slashing

down with the knife.

The End?

ABOUT THE AUTHOR

Nick Kisella grew up in Manville, New Jersey where he began writing fantasy and horror while still in high school. Some of his first published work appeared in Indie magazines during the '80s. Since then his work has appeared in various forms from print and online magazines to blogs. His first fantasy novel, 'The Emerald and the Blade' came out in 1989 by a long defunct publisher, with 'The Chalice of Souls' soon to follow. Some of his more recent work includes a screenplay and novelization for 'Nifty Entertainment' a California based Indie production company, as well as getting the first two fantasy novels he wrote as a teen, 'The Chalice of Souls' and 'Death and the Doomweaver' back in print for the sheer nostalgia of it. 'Morningstars', his first full-length horror novel was published by Black Bed Sheet Books in 2012. 'The Beasts and the Walking Dead' a post-apocalyptic fiction novel, also published by Black Bed Sheet Books is the first part of a series. He wrote the novelization to the James Balsamo film, 'I Spill Your Guts', and recently finished novelizations for Ryan Scott Weber's films, 'Mary Horror', 'Sheriff Tom versus the Zombies' and 'Witches Blood', his most recent novel. 'Crossing Lines' is the second prequel to 'The Beasts and the Walking Dead', preceded by the recent novel 'Under Construction'.

Always having an eventful life, he writes when time allows, usually after dark.

A fitness enthusiast, he has been a certified fitness instructor involved in the industry for twenty years, and continues to stay in shape and train individuals while in his late 40s.

Nick resides in Northeastern Pennsylvania with his Kimberly and their twins.

For news relating to new releases, appearances, or to purchase signed books visit:
WWW.NickKisella.com

To contact Nick Kisella look for him on Facebook :

https://www.facebook.com/nick.kisella

ABOUT THE AUTHOR

Ryan Scott Weber (Born February 24, 1980) is an
American film director, screenwriter, producer,
cinematographer, actor, editor, musician and owner
of Weber Pictures Company. Owner. He shoots and
produces many of his films in his native town of
Bernardsville, New Jersey. Ryan began his interest in
filmmaking at just 15 years old with an old VHS
camcorder. Now, at the age of 34, he is the owner of
Weber Pictures Company and Atomic Kid
Productions in New Jersey. Weber also plays the
drums and has released two albums with the Trustkill
Records band Crash Romeo in 2006 and 2008. Weber
has a distinctive directorial style. He manages to make

what look like big budget movies for little money. Weber's first feature film, Mary Horror, was released in 2012 and the sequel Sheriff Tom Vs. The Zombies in 2013. In October 2012; The Chiller Theatre Convention in Parsippany, NJ featured the film Mary Horror with two exclusive showings. In April 2013 "Sheriff Tom Vs. The Zombies" was also shown at the Chiller Theatre Convention among 9 other film festivals and Conventions. In March 2013 Weber and author Nick Kisella released the Mary Horror novel on paperback and Kindle and Nook. Sheriff Tom Vs. The Zombies the novel was released in April 2013. Weber also directed the TV SHOW "Zombies Incorporated" Season one in 2013 and the short film "The Legend Of Zeke" in 2014. Witches Blood will be also coming out in 2014. Weber Pictures will continue to make independent films and ensures us the best in yet to come!

weberpicturescompany.com

http://facebook.com/witchesblood

Witches Blood
A Weber Pictures Publication
Cover Art By Ryan Scott Weber
Nick Kisella's photo by Stan Stronski
Ryan Scott Weber's photo by Michael
Enoches Photography